STAR BINDER

By Mark Timmony

The Eye of Eternity

Starbinder
The Blood of the Spear

AN EYE OF ETERNITY NOVELLA

STAR BINDER

MARK TIMMONY

RavenHawk PUBLISHING

Starbinder

First published 2022 by Ravenhawk Publishing

This edition published by Ravenhawk Publishing
www.ravenhawkpublishing.com

ISBN: 978-0-6450965-4-5 (hardback)
978-0-6450965-5-2 (paperback)
978-0-6450965-6-9 (ebook)

Cover illustration by Felix Ortiz
Cover design by STK Kreations
Edited by Amanda J Spedding
Typeset and formatted by Zena Shapter

Australian English conventions, spelling, and grammar were used in this book.

To you, the reader.
Thank you.

CONTENTS

STARBINDER

When I first came upon the Face, I was newly raised to the rank of Seer. My cora'stone was still uncoloured, though as much a part of me as the air within my lungs.

As an initiate, I had not known the depths of Arleth'taur nor the secrets we Shaluay Starbinders kept. I had learnt of the outer world, the stars around Sobia and the history of the realms. As a Seer, I had been presented before the Probability Matrix, deemed worthy and given access to the libraries to better research and understand what I Saw.

But books are not the only thing of which the Ardes Librantus are conservators. The world within Arleth'taur, the Cradle of the Stars, contains histories as well as prophecies, works of art as well as books and scrolls, nightmares as well as dreams.

And daemons.

My daemon was trapped within the Face.

I did not know its nature when first I saw it. The quantstructs of the Shaluay often mimic life, and intelligence. I found the Face—an enormous head sculpted from metal—in a room of water, the floors and walls running with it. It rested on the floor, untouched by rust, staring at a dark ceiling and weeping red tears.

I was not meant to be in this room, but having been born to the Imperial family, I had been denied nothing and thought I knew better than my teachers.

The levels that were forbidden in Arleth'taur are the ones I sought. It was only after I Fell that I understood they were restricted with good reason.

Its voice was soft, gentle. It reminded me of the mother I had lost long ago. It enticed me, lowered my defences, and baited me with the tiniest hint of the knowledge I craved.

There is a reason the Shaluay keep their initiates sheltered, just as the Ciralys do for those who can see the Light of the Eye. But I was strong, the strongest my teachers had found in a hundred years, though in the end, I was not so strong as she who came after.

Pride. It is ever the downfall of humanity. The daemon in the Face spun its web to entice me, and I was caught without protest. I let it in, and it would not leave. It did not force me; it didn't have to. I worked with it willingly. I wanted power, and it offered that to me, as long as I allowed it to use my body, as long as I gave it the freedom to work the will of its Daemon Queen by my hand.

But it is not my story you come seeking, oh no. It is hers. She who found the Empyros and returned the Summoners to our world. She who reforged the Shaluay and reignited the Starwells. She who discovered the truth of my captor and returned it, and me, to this Face that had been built to contain it. Leaving it—leaving me—trapped here forever, a warning, a cautionary tale, that the denizens of the Void do not just seek to possess those who can wield Asai.

But it is her story you want. Not mine. No, never mine.

Come then, stranger. Sit and hear the advent of the Queen of the Stars.

CHAPTER ONE

"DON'T EVEN THINK about screaming!"

Reiana gasped as she was grabbed from behind, hands covering her eyes. "Oh, no," she said after the initial surprise had given way. "Please, don't hurt me!"

"What will you give me in exchange for letting you go?" Pren's voice, a voice as familiar to her as her own, growled in her ear.

"Well, if you let me go, I might let you eat tonight instead of stabbing you!" Reiana grabbed the dagger at her waist.

"You should stab him anyway," Esmelda said to Reiana's right. They were standing before the cauldron that sat at the centre of the caravan circle, the Heartspace of the clan. Across from them, others were drinking and talking, whittling wood or knitting as they waited for the clan hunters to return.

"Aww, that's not nice, Essie!" Pren protested with a laugh. "I made that dagger for you, Rei; you can't stab me with it."

Reiana's vision returned as Pren removed his hands from her eyes and dropped them around her waist before leaning forward and kissing her cheek.

"My name is Esmelda, or Mistress Dalna if you don't behave yourself, Prenik Hod!"

Reiana laughed at the older woman's gruff tone. Esmelda was never truly angry with anyone.

"And leave Reiana alone," Esmelda said. "None of that until you're sixteen and betrothed."

"I can't wait until I'm sixteen," Reiana said, joy filling her. "Then we can truly be together—"

"That's not going to happen." Reiana's heart sank as her grandmother joined them. "Reiana isn't for the likes of you, Prenik Hod."

Reiana turned to face the fierce old woman. Dressed in a black skirt and blouse, with a cream shawl around her shoulders and a yellow stone pendant just like Reiana's own, Relosa Milin glared at them both.

"Listening to you, Mistress Milin, Reiana isn't for the likes of anyone," Pren said, but he let Reiana go and stepped back.

"Certainly not a cripple."

"Gran!" Reiana protested.

"Don't speak back to me, girl. I raised you and you'll do what I tell you to!"

"One leg a little shorter than the other does not make Pren a cripple, Relosa," Esmelda said with a sniff.

"Mind your own business," Relosa snapped.

Esmelda shook her head. "You, of all people, should know

better, Relosa Milin." Reiana watched her smile at Pren. "I'm going to get more carrots."

Pren's cheeks flushed as he ran a hand through his dirty blonde hair. She wanted to go to him but knew better than to do so in front of her grandmother. Pren met her eyes and gave her a sad smile. Shame flooded her, and Reiana dropped her gaze. She wouldn't speak up in front of her grandmother, and what was worse, Pren wouldn't expect her to. He knew what her life was like with her grandmother. They'd talked about it often enough in the times she was able to sneak away. Guilt at her cowardice burned in her chest.

"Well," Pren said, "it's a good thing one short leg doesn't hamper me working met—"

"Raiders!" The cry came from beyond the caravans.

Across the camp, the clan dogs began to bark, and somebody screamed.

Reiana gave a start as clansfolk jumped to their feet from their places around the fire and dashed out of caravans, swords and daggers in their hands.

"Pren, no!" Reiana couldn't help protesting as she noticed the dagger he drew from the sheath at his waist.

"I have to, Rei," he said. "We all have to protect the clan."

"Yes," Relosa said. "Maybe you'll be able to stick one of them before you trip over your own feet."

Reiana looked at her grandmother, fury whipping through her. Pren touched her arm and she turned to him. He shook his head, giving her a wink, but she could see her grandmother's barb had struck home. He turned and moved off at speed, his limp barely slowing him.

"Stop mooning over that boy like a lovesick calf. Foolish girl. Get the children!" her grandmother said.

Reiana pulled her eyes away from Pren's broad back and stared across the Heartspace. "Jana has them," she said as the portly woman bustled the children who had been playing games into her wagon. Jana would keep them all safe, and her great mastiff, Keren, a fierce old dog, would guard the bolted door while Pren and the other clansfolk defended them from the raiders.

"I told you before, don't speak back to me!"

Reiana saw movement from the corner of her eye and then her head reeled, her cheek stinging and the skin heating under the imprint of her grandmother's palm, but she knew better than to cry out.

Shouts and the clash of steel came from the other side of the ringed wagons. Snarls and growls filled the air along with yelps of pain, and her mind turned to Pren. He wasn't a warrior. He'd only ever learnt the basics and spent more time with Master Korig learning to forge—

Reiana gasped as her grandmother grabbed her arm in a bruising grip, the sleeves of her thin white blouse doing as little to protect her flesh from the pincer-like fingers as it did from the chill that was rolling down the mountains as the sun set.

"Find your cousin. Make sure he's safe!"

Only when her grandmother dropped her arm, did Reiana

move; it wasn't worth the trouble that would come if she tried to back away before she'd been let go. She turned her head, silently cursing the tears that welled in her eyes. No! She'd promised herself she wouldn't cry at the things her grandmother said ever again. She wouldn't!

Reiana searched the Heartspace; the flickering light of the firepit and lanterns mingled with the rainbow-hued reflections of the stained glass of wagon windows, throwing a confusion of shadows across the space. Where was Toban? He hadn't been with the other children, and Uncle Jaril refused to take his five-year-old son with him before the clan's hunters had properly scouted this area of the New Forest. A wise move, normally, but then they hadn't expected to find raiders this close to the town of Arborfel. Unless the raiders *were* the townsfolk of Arborfel. Few folks welcomed her people, homeless since the Sundering had destroyed Nemisdrillion five hundred years ago.

No, Toban was here still. Somewhere.

The last she'd seen, he'd been near Korig's wagon, looking for—of course! Sosha was due to have her puppies today.

Reiana dashed across the Heartspace to Korig's large wagon; candles burned brightly behind its stained-glass windows and light fell out of its open door across the grass. Cries from beyond the circle of caravans rose in the air. Reiana felt the flesh on her arms pebble as the sound of ringing steel filled the air along with voices raised in anger, bellowing threats and blood curdling cries.

Heart pounding, she had just reached the wagon when

a man in uncured leather rounded the corner. His vest was studded with rusted rivets and his dirty, matted hair was pulled back in a ponytail. Stained yellow teeth grinned at Reiana through a tangled beard. The man lunged at her, blood-smeared hands reaching.

Reiana jumped back, fumbling for her dagger with numb fingers and raising it before her, a scream rising in her throat when the man yelled, his face twisting into a rictus of pain. He fell to the ground at her feet, an axe lodged in his back.

She looked up, still shocked, when Karin Dotmar appeared. The usually collected clanswoman looked wild, her eyes afire with something Reiana didn't recognise. Karin's woollen pants were stained with blood, and the azure silk scarf she usually wore was missing. Karin grabbed the handle of her throwing axe and yanked it out of the raider's back. It made a sucking sound as it was dislodged, and Reiana felt her stomach turn.

"What are ya doin' here, girl?" Karin said. "Get into a wagon. Ya gran will be worried sick!"

Reiana shook her head. "I have to find Toban."

"He'll be fine, likely the lad's already got himself a place to hide. Ya can't be out here, Reiana. I've not seen bandits like these before. They don't be from the village we passed this morning; these bastards know what they're doing."

"Pren—" Reiana started.

"He's almost a man, Rei," Karin said. "We let those we love do their duty despite the risk."

A scream came from the other side of the wagon.

Karin turned away, axe in hand. "Go, girl. Hide. Now!" Then she was off, dashing back outside the circle of the caravans.

Reiana swallowed and looked down at the dead man, her legs trembling. She wanted nothing more than to do what Karin told her, but she couldn't leave Toban out here. She just couldn't.

"Toban—" Reiana stopped at the croak that came from her throat. Clearing it, she tried again. "Toban! Where are you?"

Moving away from the dead bandit, she dropped to her hands and knees, the cool, damp grass was soft beneath her woollen skirt, and the red and gold light from the windows of the wagon catching on the blade of her dagger still in her fist and staining her hands umber. She shivered as another scream rang out and trailed off into a wet gurgling. The accented voices of men and women, strangers, called out, and she thought she recognised Helna Jabak, the wife of Atergan, the clan's best hunter, yell back in defiance.

Reiana shook her head and peered into the darkness under the wagon. "Toban!" she yelled. The other side of the wagon was washed with flickering light. Some of the torches around the encampment had been knocked over, and flames licked hungrily at the long grass, their light blinding her ability to make anything out in the shadows beneath the caravan.

"Toban!" she called again and paused as she heard the soft mewling of puppies. Sosha had birthed her litter. Toban had to be under there! Ignoring any grass stains, and what her grandmother would say about them, Reiana sheathed her dagger and crawled under the wagon. "Toban. It's me!" she hissed. "Where are you?"

"Rei?" Her cousin's soft voice came from her right.

"Toban, you have come out and get to Jana's caravan. There are bandits here!"

"Sosha had her puppies," Toban said, and Reiana could make out the golden-haired dog laying on her side with a squirming mass of black and gold pups suckling at her teats. Toban sat behind her, the orange flicker of the flames dancing over his face and across the golden furred pup in his arms.

"That's wonderful," she said, unable to hide the fear in her voice, "but you need to come with me. Grandmother sent me to get you."

"Oh," Toban said and looked up, catching her eyes. She looked away first, unable to bear the shame. Even though he was only five years of age, her little cousin was remarkably perceptive, and she could see in his gaze that he knew exactly how their grandmother had 'asked'.

"Come," she said. "Quickly, before any of the raiders think to look—"

Sosha let out a growl that raised the small hairs on the back of Reiana's neck.

"Toban," she said, her voice shaky. "Put the pup down and— *Toban!*"

A shadow ducked down to peer under the caravan and reached toward them; ruby flames sparkled across a gauntleted hand adorned with jewels on each finger as it grabbed Toban's tunic and dragged him out into the night.

Sosha's growl escalated into a bark, and she surged to her feet as Toban screamed. But Toban dropped the pup he was holding, and Reiana scooped it up, depositing with its litter mates as she scrambled out after her cousin.

The air was filled with smoke, and Reiana's eyes stung as the bitter scent seared the back of her nose, but she paid the smell and the sound of people screaming and crying little mind, focusing on the man who held Toban by the arm. A dark cloak hung from his shoulders like a shadow, and silver thread lined its edges like a sliver of moonlight. Iridescent chainmail protected his torso, and the same metal formed an intricate knot at the buckle of his belt. His armour was made of Kharidium, the lightest and strongest metal in the known world. Bandits couldn't afford Xious'bisan forged steel. More silver thread embroidered the turned-down tops of leather boots, and the rapier at his waist had a guard of luminous silver. But what struck Reiana most keenly was the wide-brimmed hat he wore, turned up on one side with a long white feather rising above it. The man looked like shadow and moonlight.

"Let me go!" Toban yelled, struggling in the man's grasp and breaking Reiana from her staring.

"Leave my cousin alone." She added her own voice to Toban's, her hand wrapping around the hilt of Pren's dagger.

The man smiled; his teeth, small and sharp and gleaming, flashed in the growing gloom. "But I've come so far to find him," he said, and again Reiana was taken by the strange quality of his accent and the way his tone made her think of summer warmth despite the chill of the night air. The man drew long fingers across Toban's cheek, gauntlet pointed like claws.

"Get away from him!" Reiana lurched forward, grabbing the man's wrist. There was a crack, and she found herself on the ground, her head ringing and her cheek throbbing from where the man had hit her.

"I don't think so, poppet," he said. "I have a contract, and I mean to see it finished."

"Reiana!" Toban cried, his struggles to pull himself free increasing until the man grabbed him by the throat and pulled him level with his face.

"Stop struggling, or I will slit your throat," he hissed, the warmth in his voice suddenly as hot as flame. Reiana couldn't see the man clearly from where she lay but whatever Toban saw in his eyes stilled her cousin instantly. "Better," the man said. He shook his head. "Human children are more trouble than they're worth. I don't care what she's paying me."

Human children? Reiana wondered at the words as she struggled to push herself upright. What other kinds of children were there? She brushed the thought aside and climbed to her feet, her cheek throbbing, blood thundering in her head. She held her dagger out before her, focusing on the man who held Toban.

"Oh, no," the man said, spinning Toban around, his arm around her little cousin's neck and the rapier that had been at the stranger's waist now drawn, its slender point aimed directly at Reiana's chest.

She blinked as the length of steel sparkled in the evening light. Even his rapier was made of Kharidium!

"You stay right there, poppet. Your cousin is coming with me."

Toban thrashed at this, and the man hissed in irritation. He spoke a word that twisted past Reiana's comprehension, and Toban went limp in his grasp.

"What have you done to him!" Reiana shouted and surged forward, the threat of the rapier forgotten.

"*Bahli an'trak!*" The man snapped. The warmth in his voice was replaced by a howling winter wind.

Reiana's lunge was arrested by a mist that suddenly swirled around her feet. Thick tendrils wrapped around her legs, clinging and holding her in place. *Asai?* The man could wield the Light of the Eye! Who was he?

"*Far* too much trouble." He sighed and smoothly returned his rapier to its scabbard, all the while juggling Toban as though the boy didn't weigh a thing.

Reiana struggled against the mist, heart racing, and lost her balance, falling forward as her feet remained in place. The mist moved along the ground, clutching at her like a pool of tar. It wrapped around her as though alive, sticky like a spider's web, and it fought against every move she made.

"Help! Pren! Karin! Help!" She cried out, looking around her, but the sounds of the fighting had shifted away from their position. The sun continued to fall behind the forest, and long shadows grew around them with no one nearby to lend aid.

"Time to go, I think." The man shifted his grip on Toban,

draping the boy over his shoulder. As he moved, his long black hair, fine as silk, pulled back from the side of his head where the brim of his hat was pinned by the white feather, revealing a pointed ear.

Blood drained from Reiana's face. "Evay!"

The Evay were fae creatures of legend, and every tale she had ever been told about them flashed through her mind. Changelings, betrayers, *child stealers*!

The man, the Evay, looked at her and smiled, his teeth needle-sharp. He gave her a half-bow, careful not to lose his grip on Toban. "Say goodbye to your cousin, poppet," the Evay said. "He's mine now."

With that, the Evay turned and jogged past the border of the caravan circle and into the trees of the surrounding forest, the white feather on his hat the only thing Reiana could see as his clothes blended into the encroaching darkness.

"No. Toban!" In a panic, Reiana strained to move forward, pulling at the mist that held her in place. She couldn't let Toban be taken. Not because of anything her grandmother might do or say but because she couldn't let him be lost to the Evay. Children taken by the Evay never returned to their families. He was her cousin by blood but her brother in all other respects. She had bathed him when he was little, had tended his cuts and scrapes—*still* tended his cuts and scrapes.

She pulled against the mist, straining with every fibre of her being. Blood pounded in her ears, her muscles taut, and her lungs burned with effort when a strange chiming sounded in her ears. At her neck flashed a pale golden light and her skin pebbled as a wave of energy washed over her. Then she was suddenly free of the mist, tumbling forward on her hands and knees.

The pendant that had belonged to her mother swung on its silver chain, its topaz stone glinting in the light of the fire. She shook her head. "Toban," she half-whispered; half cried.

Reiana looked around, but there was no one to help her. She got up, her legs shaking, though her body felt light as a feather. She didn't let herself think about her grandmother or what the woman would say or do if Reiana failed to bring Toban back. Toban was all that mattered. She had to save him. Not allowing herself to think any further, she stumbled forward, still finding her feet.

She peered into the forest in the direction the Evay had gone. He was getting away. Without another thought, she ran after him, her eyes on the white feather that bobbed through the darkening woods.

CHAPTER TWO

RELOSA WATCHED REIANA run after the creature that had Toban, and she had to lock her knees to keep from following. Instead, she turned away, unable to watch and feeling every one of her eighty-five years weighing upon her. Grasping the doorway of her caravan with one hand, she bit back her tears—just as she'd done each time she had to push Reiana away.

Relosa looked up to the night sky and stared at the stars, her body shaking.

Your fault. Your signs. Your destiny!

She closed her eyes against the diamond points of light whose prophetic arrangements had claimed Reiana's future on the day the girl had been born. "Curse the Shaluay," Relosa said and spit on the trampled grass. "And curse their stars!"

She searched for the constellations in the darkening sky, marked the Sormelene Span, an arch of rocks that belted Sobia to the north, reflecting the light of the heavens, and then made out the Herald to the east, just appearing over the horizon. It was nearing time.

"Why? Why take my little Reiana?" Relosa shook her head. "She was all I had left of my daughter."

Breathing deeply, she removed her clenched fingers from the doorframe. There was no use cursing the stars. If Sharné, that cold bitch goddess of the Stars, had chosen her granddaughter, who was Relosa to bewail the will of the Elder Gods?

Who was she? No one. Just an old woman, called wise by some. A survivor of fallen Nemisdrillion lost beneath the New Sea. One of those called the Wanderers on this sundered realm.

"Yes, *Wanderers*." She snorted. "Thieves of cattle and horses. Defilers of children. Doomed of the Sunlord. Bah!"

It was *her* people who kept the old ways alive. It was her mother, and her mother's mother, and her great-great-grandmother who had passed on the knowledge of their ancestors for the sake of their people in this changed world. A world still wracked by the War of the Summoners and the Sundering some five hundred years past. The great cities were now gone, though the Var worked to restore what order they could. At least the Hyla'var and their Imperium did not send her people away when they approached the new cities. But their example did not go far enough to change the men and women inside those city's walls. The rulers of the *noble* houses had already begun to demand tribute, ignoring the laws the Var had put in place.

The Var and their great congress would fall too. She had seen it.

And of all those humans scrambling in the dust, claiming to have the blood of the Summoners—as if that gave them the right to nobility and not a death sentence—it was her granddaughter, a Wanderer, who would lead an Empyros to save them all when the Daemon Queen came again. It would be a *Wanderer* who would lead the way out of an age of darkness and into a new age of glory.

She looked over her shoulder at Korig's caravan, but Reiana had long since disappeared into the forest. "May the Mother shelter you, the Stars speak to you, and the Eye of Eternity bless your path, my child," she said.

Sighing, she stepped through the entry and closed the door. Inside the caravan stretched shelves piled high with scrolls and racks filled with jars of potions, poultices, and spices. Fat beeswax candles sat in silver holders on every available space. Intricately carved Amarian chests and boxes of cedar—inlaid with precious metals and rare stones—were tucked under benches and pushed into corners. And on the ceiling was a painstakingly drawn chart of the night sky. The Thirteen Houses of the heavens and their many constellations were rendered to scale and outlined by a border depicting the phases of the moon.

Moving through the chaotic arrangement, Relosa made her way towards the back half of the caravan where her worktable was positioned in front of a throne-like chair of rosewood and velvet cushions. The table was odd, its surface a black mirror-like finish. It was unlike anything she'd ever seen. It had come with them from the Old World, from lost Nemisdrillion, and it was the key to her power as a Stargazer.

Lowering her weary bones into the chair, Relosa rested her head in her hands and allowed herself one last moment of self-pity for the cruel task she'd had to carry out over the last fifteen years. And for Reiana, who was the innocent recipient of that cruelty.

"But it had to be," she said and firmly pushed herself upright. "It was foretold. Her destiny will be greater than her people's. If I hadn't prepared her for what is to come, then she would have failed her task."

Around her, Relosa felt the spirits of her mother and grandmother and all the wise women who had lived in the caravan before her, and an insidious thought crept in. *But was it enough?*

Relosa dismissed the thought with a wave of her hand. "I have given her lessons to strengthen her and to help her survive in this broken world. I have taught her of the Tidal Lanes and the Star Paths. I have told her of our ancestors and Erth, and I have taught her the constellations. It will have to be enough."

Relosa closed her eyes and prayed for strength from any of the Elder Gods listening. She wasn't an initiated Starbinder; but she would do what she could. What she must. There was no one else. The signs were clear, and they all confirmed the foretelling that had come upon her fifteen years ago.

"Born is the Queen of the Stars. To Sharné she is called,

and to the Starmaster she is to be sent. To the keepers of the knowledge she is entrusted, to the Starwell, she is bound. Forged in betrayal, tempered by the stellar wind, she will lead the people from the age of darkness and hold in her hands their salvation. Summon the Last to her via the Third Lane as the Herald enters the First House."

Tonight, the Herald would enter the First House of the heavens.

Relosa steeled herself. She had no time for doubts. She, the daughter of a Wanderer, a Stargazer, would do as the stars bid and harness their powers to call the Starmaster of the Shaluay.

If such a person still lived.

For five hundred years, the world had received no aid from the Shaluay. Relosa found it difficult to believe that if any Starbinders remained, they would have hidden away from a world in desperate need of the guidance for which their Order was renowned. The Shaluay were healers, seers, and advisors; servants to the Lady of the Stars, not power mad Ciralys binding their lives to the Eye of Eternity and living for centuries.

Bah! You sit here dawdling while your granddaughter chases a treacherous creature to face a destiny of which she has no idea. Do your part, woman!

Twisting in her chair, she reached across the table for a box of Sahrin design, inlaid with carvings of the constellations. Opening the box carefully, she removed a crystal orb no larger than the palm of her hand.

"Is that a Starstone?" a dry voice asked from behind her. "I've never seen one before."

Relosa dropped the orb back into its box and slammed the lid, the wards flaring as they reactivated, and she spun to face the intruder.

Behind her, standing before the bed at the back wall of the caravan—where no one had been a moment ago—was a man, a *creature*, dressed in black, a broad-brimmed hat, one side pinned up by a white feather.

"Tsk, tsk," he said. A smile played on thin lips, but Relosa saw his eyes narrow in anger. "I was only asking."

"Your kind never 'only asks'," Relosa snapped back. "What are you doing here? You are meant to be leading my granddaughter—"

"Yes, yes." The creature waved his hand dismissively, ruby stones flashing on gauntleted fingers. "She is currently chasing me through the forest to the ruins you chose."

"How can she be following you when you are here?" Relosa spat, rising to her feet.

A delicate eyebrow lifted above one eye; the pupil slit like a cat's. "She follows what she *thinks* is me. The shadows in the forest are too dark to see anything clearly, but the feather in my hat is quite luminescent in the dark. Of course, it's not the feather in my hat she follows but a ghost owl. It will lead her where you want her to go."

"Our bargain was for you to lead her yourself!"

"Our *bargain* was nothing of the sort. Choose your words more carefully when dealing with my kind, Wanderer. You demanded that your granddaughter be led to the ruins, and being led there she is. You did not specify that I do it myself. And given you also demanded that your grandson be returned to you…"He turned with a flare of his cloak, revealing Toban asleep on the bed behind him."I judged my time better spent returning him here *before* your hunters arrive and finish off the rest of the rabble your coins bought."

"*Evay*," Relosa said. "Always twisting the nature of a bargain."

The creature hissed, drawing upright and towering over her. The glamour he wore fell away like black smoke. A mane of white hair spread from his head, and a red-lipped mouth of needle-sharp teeth revealed itself on a face of ash-grey skin, the light of the candles found crimson eyes that seemed to flare as they took Relosa in. His clothes fell away like shadows fleeing from the light revealing a well-muscled chest and a single pauldron, a skull of some sort gracing his left shoulder. A belt of gold coins hung at his waist above black silk trousers tucked into knee-high boots capped with more bone-white skulls. The transformation caught the breath in her throat, and Relosa reached instinctively for the pendant at her neck.

"I am Dasha'vay, *human*, as well you know. Do not call me Evay again. I left my cousins long ago. You will call me *Zhalon-kena*." Red eyes dropped to her lined hand clutching the pendant."And your little charm does not have the strength to stop me if I wanted to change our bargain."

Relosa narrowed her eyes. *Zhalon-kena*? Great Master? Not with the last breath in her body. Titles, like names, had power amongst the Evay, and she'd offer him none. As for changing the bargain. No, he could no more do that than any Evay could, no matter how far down the path of the Void he'd travelled.

She dropped her hand from the topaz at her neck. She didn't need the pendant. "No, Zurzic," Relosa said, "I don't believe I will. You are bound by the terms of our bargain, and I shall not be changing them."

"But think of what you might receive in exchange." If her refusal to address him as Zhalon-kena annoyed him, Zurzic didn't show it. "Don't your bones ache, your aged body pain you? I could relieve you of the infirmities of your mortality."

"No!" Relosa shook her head. "I will not hear it. You were charged to lead my granddaughter to the Starwell—"

"*Starwell?* A temple to Sharné? And you with a Starstone no less. So, the Shaluay stir? What is it about your granddaughter that so interests the Starbinders, hmmm?"

"You should have sought the answer to that question before you agreed to the bargain. Did you really imagine that a Stargazer of the Wanderers would exile one of their own lineage? I had thought better of the Evays—your pardon—*Dasha'vays* cunning."

Zurzic surged toward her, and the wards set into the floor around the table flared to life, halting him in his tracks.

"Filthy creature," she spat. "You cannot touch me here, not in the seat of my own power. I have a mind to end you now and rid the world of one more voidsworn."

"You cannot," Zurzic said with a laugh like the rustle of

dead leaves in autumn. "The bargain binds you as well as it does me."

"Only until I give you your payment."

"Yes, my payment. Show me." Zurzic's eyes flared in hunger, and this time she could not pretend the inner fire was a reflection of the candlelight.

Relosa swallowed, revulsion twisting inside her. She did what she had to do.

She turned from the fallen Evay and glanced at the table; its black mirrored surface was devoid of marking but for a tiny sigil, flashing red. Time was running out. She reached for a small flask sitting beside the chest that held the Starstone, her eyes sliding off the dark liquid within lest the memories escape the cell she'd consigned them to.

"Your payment, daemon. Blood soaked in the light of the dark moon. And not the blood of any of my own clan, so do not think you will have a hold on any of my people."

"It had best be human blood, or our bargain is null—"

"Yes, yes." She spoke over him. "It is human blood. Life blood, as you demanded."

"And the body of the child from which it came?"

Relosa's heart beat hard in her chest. "Buried. You will not find it."

"A shame," he said.

Relosa didn't bother hiding her disgust. "Let us finish this." She tossed him the flask, and he snatched it out of the air.

"And *done*," Zurzic said. His lips curled, and he glanced to the side, down at Toban still asleep on the bed. "The child's body would have been useful, but I can always use this one instead—"

Relosa turned to the table and slapped her palm down on the flashing red sigil.

The Shaluay artifact activated.

Lines of orange light appeared on the table's mirror-like finish, and more sigils appeared around its edges. And as the table activated, so did the wards in her caravan. The Dasha'vay's movement was arrested once more as a circle of white light appeared around him.

"What is this?" Zurzic snarled, straining against the confines of the light but unable to pass its perimeter. "What have you done, Witch?"

"I am protecting my own," Relosa said. "Our bargain is done, and you are not welcome here. Begone!"

At her words, the light began to contract around the creature, brightening in intensity until, with a flash, it was gone. So was the Dasha'vay.

Relosa slumped against the table. Never again would she work with such a creature. *Never.* But she'd been left little choice here.

No-one in the New World would help the Wanderers, and her son would never countenance Reiana being sent to Starbinders as she needed to be. Relosa was too old to take the girl there herself. And her own feelings for the child bore no resemblance to the ones she'd been forced to show her granddaughter.

Reiana, forgive me!

It had been all she could do over the years to stop the girl forming attachments to the clan, to her family.

The caravan became blurry, and Relosa wiped her eyes.

The foretelling bound her as surely as it did Reiana. It had to be done.

Relosa shuffled over to the bed to check on Toban. She put her hand on his forehead. He was unharmed. She cupped his cheek. That he'd been put in danger for this escapade… she shook her head. He was safe. That was the important thing.

Relosa straightened. She had work to do.

———•———

Zurzic appeared outside of the ring of caravans. Night had fallen over the grove that the Stargazer Relosa had her clan stop in so he could enact his part of their bargain. He was not one to waste his time for a vial of human blood, newborn or not, but the Stargazer had known the words to summon him and knew his name to bind him. He had been unable to refuse.

If he'd been able to take her grandson from her, he would feel more well appeased than he did with a single flask of a newborn's dark moon-soaked blood. But she was better prepared than he'd expected—and he *should* have expected it of one who knew the ritual of binding! He had not been compelled by a human in over five hundred years. And if he hadn't been exploring the changes wrought to this plane since the War of the Summoners, he'd have not been bound now.

But, as with all such ancient cants, he could not be bound again once they were used and the bargain met. As so many Summoners had discovered to their peril.

A voice came from within the circled wagons. The bandits he'd recruited for the diversion the Stargazer had demanded had already been dealt with. His lip curled in a snarl. Human filth.

The sound faded, the person moving away, and the tension left him, but the banked flames of his rage did not. Zurzic's eyes narrowed as he considered. He need not take the hag's grandson to cause her grief for the effrontery of binding him.

In his hand appeared the kharidium rapier he'd held at the throat of the granddaughter.

No human, at least none amongst these Wanderers, could stand against one of the Dasha'vay. He would show her what it meant to treat him with such contempt. He would see their Heartspace bathed in blood while the Stargazer huddled in her caravan!

Zurzic strode forward only to be flung back toward the forest as wards formed by the iron-poled torches the clan set around their camp flared to life, refusing him entry. He couldn't hold back the cry as he crashed into a tree, slumping to the forest floor, blood trickling from his mouth.

Voices rose again from within the camp, and Zurzic bit off a curse. He pulled the shadows of the forest around himself like a cloak as two women peered into the darkness from the edge of the nearest caravan.

He cursed the old hag silently.

The women soon left, retreating into the circle of the caravans, and Zurzic got to his feet.

The shadows he'd used to hide in fell away like mist before the sun, and he walked the edge of caravans in silence until he came upon two corpses. Looking them over, he chose one, a blond-haired clan boy with a ragged-edged gut wound, the boy's hands frozen at his belly, trying to hold his intestines in behind the sword slash that had killed him. Kneeling in the shadows beside the dead human, Zurzic yanked the hands away from the gaping wound and spit into it. Then, he unstoppered the flask of newborn blood and poured thirteen drops into the dead boys gaping stomach.

Closing his eyes, Zurzic opened himself to *Des'maadr* and allowed the dark light of the Void to flow through him. With barely a thought, he wielded the power through the twisted runes he envisioned in his mind's eye. Bending over the corpse, he whispered in its ear.

"Ak boltah, delak nes dray!"

The chill of the night plunged to freezing, and frost crackled over the boy's body, crystals of frozen blood sparkling in the light of the warded torches.

The skin around the boy's stomach began to bulge, to move, as something inside him struggled to get out.

Zurzic stood, stepping out of the way as the voidspawn's struggles to escape ended in an explosion of wet, popping sounds; chunks of cadaver and black blood struck the side of the caravan facing the woods as thirteen immature borewyrms slid out of the corpse.

Borewyrms had been used by the Dark Summoners during the war; pulled from the Void, they could only survive in this world by feeding on *Asai*, but he'd attuned these wyrms to human blood. They wouldn't live long at all on that, but they'd last long enough to kill every man, woman, and child in this wretched clan. The maggot-like pallor of their flesh glowed white under the light of the moon, and Zurzic smiled.

A dog barked. The borewyrms turned toward the sound. Blind they might be, but their hearing was acute. As was their hunger. The segmented white bodies began to move; the sucker-like mouths, lined with needle-sharp teeth, opened and closed as they went hunting for human blood.

He laughed. The Stargazer was a fool to think she could bind a Dasha'vay with impunity.

Turning, Zurzic faced the forest. Now, he couldn't kill the granddaughter, the bargain—though complete—still held some things sacrosanct. But he could stop her from reaching the Shaluay. And if he foiled some scheme of the Starbinders as well as the old woman's, so much the better.

He made to move but stopped as a thought struck him.

He glanced back down at the dead boy, the exit of the wyrms had moved his face into a stream of torchlight that sparkled in his dead, blue eyes. *Yes*, Zurzic thought. *Why do the deed myself when one of her clan can do it?*

Kneeling beside the corpse, Zurzic sunk his hands into the hard-packed soil of the forest floor as though it was water. He dug great clots of dirt from the ground and poured them into the gaping cavity of the boy's torso. Wielding *Des'maadr*, he traced runes in violet light above the body.

"Umbeth nak der. Azh ghul nok sinj. Dak ron mah!"

The runes flared once and sunk into the corpse, pulling skin over the hole in his stomach until just a jagged incision running from sternum to groin remained. The blue eyes flared with purple light before returning to their natural hue, and the body rose in jerking, unnatural motions, animated by the power of the Void.

Zurzic studied it as it stood, a slight tilt to its posture. He looked down and noted the body's knees were not in alignment. One leg was shorter than the other.

"Humans," Zurzic said. "Only they would allow a deformity to live past infancy."

Summoning *Des'maadr* once more, shadows coalesced in the forest, hiding the trees and branches as all light was banished. Zurzic gestured for his ghul to proceed him into the dark maw and then followed, disappearing as the first screams rose from within the circle of caravans behind them.

Settling herself, Relosa leant back in her chair. That she'd been forced to deal with a void-tainted creature sickened her. And the things she'd had to do to complete their bargain made her want to howl in anguish. But she had no time for recriminations. Reiana would be approaching the Starwell soon, and the stars continued to turn in the heavens, uncaring of the troubles of mortals below them.

Relosa took a breath and pushed the Dasha'vay and the requirements of tonight's actions from her mind. She focused on her breathing, clearing her mind of distractions, ignoring the sounds of the clan outside. The hunting party would be returning soon, and they would assist in cleaning up any remaining bandits.

Placing her hand on the Sahrin-made box, she withdrew the Starstone once more.

Relosa stared into the palm-sized orb, tracing the natural latticework of cracks, watching the glow of the candles as the refracted light chased itself around the inner maze. The vibrations of the crystal ran through her hand, its energy brushing against her.

After a moment, she set the Starstone on the table. A new line of light appeared on the mirror-black surface, tracing itself around the orb, and lines spread out from that circle marking the thirteen houses of the heavens, the orb at their centre. At the cardinal points around the circle, sigils representing north, south, east, and west appeared in the same orange light and began to blink, a pulsing that increased in speed until it seemed to be a steady glow.

Relosa watched the sequence with some small amount of awe. She could recall the first time she'd seen this wonder as a girl; she had wanted to run and get her father, her brother, to show the whole clan this sight but her mother had sworn her to secrecy before she began to impart the teachings her own mother had passed on to her.

More lines of light appeared on the tabletop, these ones representing the veins of energy that flowed across Sobia, echoing the slow shift of the Sormelene Span that bisected the heavens east to west, the orbit of the moon and the turning of Sobia itself. As the lines shifted across the table, she waited until one—the line representing the Third Tidal Lane—came to a stop near the Starstone orb. She moved the orb, rolling it across the table; the lines of light beneath moved with it until the Stone was sitting directly upon the line of the Tidal Lane. Then she touched the orb with her right forefinger. Centring her mind, Relosa reached out with her thoughts, completing her link to the orb, and through the ancient table, to the power of the Third Tidal Lane.

Relosa stifled a scream as her mind's eye opened. She was falling, spinning, as her consciousness was swept into the labyrinthine structure of cracks and natural imperfections in the Starstone's crystal framework. The gentle yellow glow of captured candlelight exploded into a million stars of blinding light that receded quickly into deep indigo, echoing the night sky outside the caravan. There was no after image for her to blink away, and the forces raised by the table and her amateur conjuring swiftly carried her consciousness up into the stellar winds that swept across the universe.

She grabbed hold of the reins of her sanity, panic sharpening into a desperate focus as the power of the Third Lane threatened to rip away the fabric of her mind. Desperation was all that kept her sane. Desperation and the knowledge that if she failed in this sending, she had sentenced Reiana to a short, empty existence.

And the world to disaster.

She thought again of the foretelling that had come upon her at Reiana's birth. The foretelling that had consumed her attention as her daughter lay dying on the birthing bed. Grasping at the words that had haunted her for fifteen long years.

"Born this night is the Queen of the Stars ..."

Relosa tried to speak the words, to call out, seeking in them some tether to sanity, but the power washed over her, buffeted her, drowned her small voice with the music of the stars' singing light. She cursed as she searched her memory for the words she needed. She was no Shaluay Starbinder to try this. Yes, she had the knowledge but not the experience. Her experiments with the Starstone were limited to foretelling and scrying. Not reaching into the tides of the stars themselves!

The power of the Third Tidal Lane flared around her, roaring through her senses, racing along her nerves like liquid fire. Relosa held on with all her might as the explosion of sound marking the arrival of the Herald into the First House erupted in her mind—and with it came the words she needed.

Struggling, she set her voice on the stellar winds and forced the words out with the sheer strength of her will.

Done! she cried silently, her mind imprinting on the Tidal Lane. *Delivered unto you, Starmaster, is the daughter of a*

Stargazer! In the fifteenth year of her life, the Herald proclaims her. Your Star Queen comes!

Relosa felt the stellar winds take her words and fling the resonance of their vibrations across the Third Tidal Lane in a flaring storm.

CHAPTER THREE

VENDRAN SABAY, STARMASTER of the Order of the Shaluay Starbinders, stood on the balcony of his private rooms high in Arleth'taur and watched the shower of meteors flare in the night sky as the Herald entered the First House.

"It is time," he said, though no one was there to hear him. For nearly seven centuries he had been marked with the white hair—the sign of the Shaluay as surely as the Khaderneous was the sign of the Summoners—and for four of those centuries, he'd held the rank of Starmaster, one of the few men to ever do so. In that time, he had always kept the politics of the Order away from his rooms. These chambers, looking south across the emptiness of a desert of black sands, had remained his shelter, his refuge, his sanctum from the day-to-day politicking of the Order. Only his personal servants might have heard him, but none of them knew he had awoken from stasis.

Vendran turned and walked through the large arched

doorways, the chill winds of the night blowing in off the desert behind him. Four hundred years ago, before the Sundering, the desert outside had been the Su'ji Forest, but then the skies rained fire for months on end, and the forest died, leaving only black sands behind. The only green for leagues was along the Lunsa River that threaded through the desert from Waolin to Shi'a Li'ang.

He moved through the formal sitting room. Crystal wall globes glowed softly in response to his movement, revealing plush Sorentian chairs and couches and low white stone tables from Ki'ren. The furnishings were a small reminder of both cities that had been destroyed when the Vanya Mountains fell during the War of the Summoners. Silver-toned wood sparkled on the walls, carved with fabulous beasts and flowers. The wood had come from the great Silvanar trees that had once populated the Su'ji Forest. Vendran had been told by the emissaries of the Celestial Court in Shi'a Li'ang that only the Empress herself had such panels now. Their inference being that the Shaluay should turn over all the Silvanar wood in Arleth'taur to her; he had refused. But it was the starscene chart hanging in its frame and taking up almost an entire wall that he stopped before. Meticulously calculated from hours in a Probability Trance, the Star Paths and Tidal Lanes it mapped had been wrought with exquisite detail. Vendran had waited so long for its alignment, for this child to be sent to the Shaluay, that he had almost stopped believing it would come to pass.

Vendran scoffed to himself. Foolishness. He had calculated

the branches of the Probability Tree himself; he knew what could come, what *would* come, better than anyone.

With a thought, he linked with the Amethyst cora'stone in the silver torque around his neck and the old Nemisdrillionese Stargazers words, flung into the Third Tidal Lane, played over in his mind. He concentrated on them again and then looked deeper. This Stargazer of the Wanderers, this Relosa, had no formal training, and beneath the words rang the foretelling that guided her to this outcome: *"Born this night is the Queen of the Stars. To the keepers of the knowledge she is entrusted, and to the Starwell she is bound."*

There was more, but that was enough. It matched Vendran's own mapping of the future in the first years after the Sundering when the great civilisation the Summoners had built crumbled into the New Sea, and millions had perished.

"One spark in the darkness is all we need to light our way, to guide us, and to rekindle what we have lost."

Vendran shook himself. There was no time to dawdle. A darkness had touched the edges of the old woman's call. A resonance of the Void. He needed to get to the Astroglade now or else this child, this keystone to the Starscroll Prophecies and humanity's future, might be lost.

He turned away from the starscene and crossed the room to an alcove containing a circular platform. Vendran stood upon the platform and directed a single thought at his cora'stone to activate the teleport. His private chambers disappeared from his sight as he was instantly transported to another platform forty floors below.

The hallways of the Star Cradle were dark, another indicator that the Shaluay's ranks had thinned as drastically as those of the Ciralys, perhaps more so. But Vendran needed little light to find his way in this place that had been his home since he was eleven years old, and he swiftly made his way down a corridor to the Astroglade.

Passing through the wide doors that slid open silently before him and walking into the glade, Vendran came to a stop.

Located in the heart of Arleth'taur, the Astroglade was a circular room over six hundred feet in diameter; its vaulted ceiling reached two hundred feet in height at its peak. Around the room's edge ran an expansive observation deck called the Starseer's Rise, with a single walkway reaching out to the Skydeck, a platform floating one hundred feet above the giant Starwell in the centre of the glade. On the Skydeck rested the Star Altar, the heart of the Astroglade.

Vendran had expected the Astroglade to be inert, but the great star chart was alive in the air above the Altar, depicting the night sky above Arleth'taur in intricate detail. And on the Skydeck stood a single figure in the silver robes of a Senior Binder, her long platinum hair pulled back off her face with diamond combs.

"Arais," he said. "I did not expect to see you."

Arais Sometsu, daughter of the Imperial House that ruled Amaria, turned and offered him a bow. "It is my turn to watch the initiates, Starmaster," she said. "One of the quantstructs notified me that your sleep chamber was empty."

"And you thought to check on me?" He came up beside her. The Starwell below was dark, as it had been since the Sundering.

"It is a difficult time we find ourselves in," Arais said. "I wished only to see that you were well and if there was anything I could be of assistance with."

"I am in good health, child," Vendran told her. "Have any of the seekers returned with news of the Matrix?"

"No, Starmaster." Arais looked at him, her silver Amarian eyes almost glowing against her blue skin. "The Estay Matrix is still lost to us."

"And so, the other Starwells remain silent." Vendran nodded and passed his hand over the Star Altar. A sigil flared on the crystal surface in bright lines of white light, and stars began to fill the Starwell below—blue, green, red, white, and yellow stars glowed next to those of amethyst, gold and silver.

Arais shrugged. "For the most part, yes."

"Indeed. For the most part. And the Tal'adin?"

"You were correct. What remains of the Tal'adin Order has disbanded. Some have joined the ranks of royal households; others have banded together in the north around the Towers of the Stars."

Vendran turned to look at her, eyebrows raised. "The Towers? I did not see that. It may… complicate things if they settle in."

"They are led by one calling themself the Paladine," Arais said.

"I see." Vendran turned back to the well, considering. "What of the Ciralys?"

"Some of the Tal'adin have remained, but they now call themselves the Tal'desai."

"And so, they fracture." Vendran shook his head. "Has the emissary from Shi-Kaan arrived yet?"

It was Arais' turn to stare at him. "How did you... That is, yes, Starmaster. The Blay Shon have approached us with a... I had planned to write it up in my report for the next gathering of the Collective."

"By all means. Their offer is genuine and will benefit the Shaluay greatly in this New World."

Arais was silent for a moment as though weighing her words. "Starmaster, may I ask why you have awoken? The Collective is not due to convene again for another five years."

"I am aware, daughter. My waking was required. A new candidate comes to the Shaluay tonight."

"Surely the Seneschal can deal with that? You have not tested a candidate for many years."

Vendran laughed. "You mean centuries. But no, the Seneschal cannot deal with her as she does not approach Arleth'taur. She comes to us from the sixty-eighth complex."

"The sixty-eighth— But that is in the third quadrant." Arais could not hide her surprise. "How can she... you plan to link to the well? But the wells are silent."

"There is power enough for this," Vendran said.

"And this candidate is worth the risk?"

"Tell me, Arais, in the five hundred years since the

Sundering, how many new candidates have arrived at Arleth'taur?"

"Since Amaria closed their borders and the Complexes have been silent? Maybe fifty."

"Fifty-four," Vendran said, his eyes still on the Starwell as the stars in its boundaries shifted and danced. "And how many of our Order have been lost in the upheaval?"

He felt her eyes on him as she answered. "I believe one hundred thousand cora'stones have gone dark in the Swarm at last count."

Vendran met her silver gaze. "You answer your own question. Yes, a new candidate is worth this effort. This candidate most of all. The Shal'ashay must be taught to those who will best lead humanity forward."

"You have Seen."

"Yes," Vendran said. "I have Seen. During the last meeting of the Collective, I looked into the Starwell and engaged the Probability Matrix. She will lead us all into the future."

Something sparked in the back of Arais' eyes at his words, but she turned her face away and nodded. "As the stars turn."

He studied her profile for a moment, but he had no more time. Arais was talented; that was undeniable. And as a member of House Sometsu, she had also been born with ambition in her blood. A dangerous combination. She was destined to rank amongst the First Tier of the Collective, but she would never lead them.

"Stand ready," he told her. "I will commune with the well."

Vendran closed his eyes, linking with the cora'stone at his

neck. With the ease of long practise, he tuned its power to the song of the stars in the well below.

The words of the Stargazer on the other side of the New Sea touched his awareness like a gentle draft from a closing door. An initiate of lesser rank would have missed the words of the woman who so recklessly attempted to ride the force of the Third Tidal Lane as it began to peak toward its ascendency. Still, he plucked out the vibrations that were the woman's words from the raging torrent of power and let them sear across his mind's eye.

"Delivered unto you, Starmaster is the child of a Stargazer! In the fifteenth year of her life, the Herald proclaims her coming. Your Star Queen is given to you!"

Vendran felt an outpouring of gratitude and relief swell within him at the words, and he reached for the old woman's awareness. Even now, she was unravelling as the primal forces of the Lane began to burn her mind away. With a single thrust of his will, he disentangled her from the peril she had placed herself in, and as his awareness brushed against her own, their minds locked together.

Vendran frowned, feeling his cora'stone pulse as a vortex of memories, emotions and knowledge about the girl who would one day inherit the mantle of Starmaster flooded his mind through the link.

Holding the image of the girl—Reiana—in his mind, he sent the diamond-hard strength of his focused attention spinning along the lightways of the stars to the blank absence he sensed in the starsong within the forest that surrounded the Wanderers' camp. Tapping the power of the Third Tidal Lane, he opened a conduit and reached his mind through the Starwell in the Astroglade, casting a sequence of sigils to ignite the Starwell in the ruins of the sixty-eighth complex that had lain dormant for the last five hundred years.

CHAPTER FOUR

TRUE NIGHT FELL, and the shadows of the forest deepened. Only the faintest spears of light filtered through the canopy, but it was enough for Reiana to leap logs and tree roots. Mostly. Somewhere in the distance, a wolf howled, and she tripped over a dip in the ground, slamming down on the packed soil of the forest floor. Pushing herself up, she took a moment, breathing hard before continuing; the white feather bobbing in the distance ahead of her remained tantalisingly out of reach yet never disappeared.

"I hope you are tripping over every tree root as well, you bastard!" Reiana hissed to herself, making her way forward more cautiously. Though she was warm from running, a chill crept up her spine, and she adjusted the tied shawl around her shoulders. Having passed through the forest in daylight, she knew there were large tracts of open ground between the trees, but the shrubs and bushes that also shared the space made for treacherous obstacles in the dark. And the local wildlife that called the forest home made strange chittering noises in the night that chilled her blood.

"Grandmother's right," she said. "I'm useless. Why didn't I bring a torch?"

Breathing heavily, she took in the scent of leaves, bark, flowers, and dirt. The rich, earthy aroma carried hints of damp and mold. She eyed her surroundings warily and wrapped her right hand around the hilt of the dagger Pren had crafted for her. By the High God Orthias and all the Elder Gods, why couldn't Pren be with her now?

She shook her head. No. She could do this. She *must* do this. Toban depended on her, and she needed to do her part in looking after the clan as much as Pren did.

Still, who knew what was buried in these woods? Athmay was not a safe place. It hadn't been since the War of Summoners and the Sundering five hundred years earlier. Nemisdrillion, an entire realm, the home of her people, had been lost beneath the sea, leaving her ancestors to roam, seeking somewhere to settle. But when they weren't being attacked by the daemons that still hunted in the wilds, they were chased away by people who blamed Nemisdrillion for the Sundering.

Reiana didn't understand how her people could be blamed for the Sundering. They weren't Summoners. She shook her head. It was no good thinking about such things. The clans did what they could to survive; they cared for one another, protected each other. If Pren could face bandits in the clan's defence, she could chase down one who'd taken her cousin!

She wiped her eyes with the back of her hand. There was no time for tears. She had to catch up to the Evay. Not that she had any idea what she'd do when did, she just had to get Toban back.

What an Evay was doing with the bandits, she didn't know. Every story she'd heard of them said they shunned humans. Though they did take children from their beds... but they usually left a changeling in their place. Nothing had been left in Toban's place, had it?

She kept moving, the moonlight shifting down through tree branches and leaves was more treacherous than it was helpful, but she pushed her way forward, trying not to lose her footing again.

The white of the feather in the Evay's hat drifted ahead of her still, enticing her. She quickened her pace and promptly tripped, sprawling on the forest floor again. Her palms stung, but she couldn't see if she'd just grazed them or if they were bleeding in the dark.

She couldn't see anything! She should have brought a torch with her instead of just running off like the fool girl her grandmother was always calling her. Tears welled again, and her chest tightened as fear threatened to overwhelm her. Her arms shook, and a tremor wracked her frame.

No! I can do this. I can.

She grasped the topaz pendant dangling at her neck. It had been her mother's. At least that's what her grandmother told her. It was a twin to the one her grandmother wore and was said to have been passed down in the family since before Nemisdrillion fell. Reiana liked to think that her mama watched over her when she wore it, and she rarely took it off.

Reiana took a breath.

And then she took another, reaching deep within her, looking for that calm space that she would flee to when her grandmother's scolding became too much to bear.

I can.

I just need some *light*.

With the thought came the same chiming sound she'd heard as she'd broken free of the Evay's enchantment back at the camp. And with the chime came a swell of energy, like a burst of adrenaline. A soft yellow radiance lit the forest before her. Looking down, she gasped. Her mother's pendant floated before her, pulling on its chain and glowing with light.

Hesitantly she touched the stone. It was neither hot nor cold, and it just hung in the air before her. It had never done that before.

Her grandmother had never mentioned it could do this.

Afraid to lose the pendant—and its unexplained light—Reiana got to her feet, keeping the necklace on lest the stone float away. She moved forward once more, careful to keep her eyes off the stone to retain her night vision, and locked them on the white feather bobbing in the darkness ahead. The feather was moving farther away but now that the roots of trees and the clawing grasp of the shrubs were revealed, she managed to increase her pace without falling.

The sudden flapping of wings and a hoot in the dark had her whirling around, her dagger in hand and held out before her until her mind caught up with the racing of her heart. An owl. It must have been an owl.

"At least there are no daemoncats out here," she said to herself. "I hope."

Turning back around, she had just started forward again when the white feather in the distance ahead of her suddenly disappeared.

"No, no, no!" Reiana grasped her skirts in her other hand and ran. It didn't take long before she burst out of the cover of the trees onto the slope of a hill covered in long grass. She could make out white flowers swaying amongst the shadowy blades in the night breeze, and the trickle of water—a stream running across the base of the hill—reflected the light from her pendant. It was like a border, this strip of land between the tall trees behind her and the thick-boled ancients that rose in the forest ahead of her. To her right, she could see snow-capped mountains in the south, and in the night sky to the left, she had an unhindered view of the Sormelene Span that girded the heavens in the north.

A spark of light caught her attention, and Reiana looked up to see a blaze of meteors seemingly explode from the constellation of the Herald, and with them, she heard that strange chiming again.

She shook her head and lowered her eyes from the display. She had to find Toban. "The Evay had to have kept going. It couldn't just disappear, could it?" Actually, considering all the stories she'd heard about the Evay, they probably could just up and disappear!

Reiana scanned the line of trees and cupped her hand around the light of the pendant when she realised it was no longer glowing. She looked at the stone in surprise; in the light of the moon, its colour was a washed-out grey. She didn't know how she had made the light shine from it—if she had been the one to make it do anything at all—and she didn't understand why it had ceased to glow now, but she was very grateful that it had led her this far.

Letting go of the pendant, it fell back onto her chest, and Reiana looked around the forest, squinting into the shadows.

There! A flash of white a little to the northeast. The feather. She dashed down the hill and jumped the small stream.

This stretch of the forest seemed older, darker than the one she'd just run through, and she felt like she was moving through smears of shadow in black, greys and ghostly whites. The space between these trees was wider, and she increased her pace, chasing the Evay, her lungs burning. She only slowed as she noticed a strange glow coming from the trees ahead. Where was the Evay taking Toban?

The clearing opened before her, wider even than the Heartspace of the clan. With care, she moved into the deeper shadows, slowly making her way forward until she could see past the forest into an enormous glade. Great blocks of stone—marble or everstone?—lay strewn across the forest floor. Grass and weeds reached up through cracks in what looked to be some sort of paving, and large clumps of phosphorus moss glowed on the stumps of columns that lay half-buried in the ground.

Reiana froze, her skin prickling as her eyes fell on what looked like a small body lying splayed on the paving ahead of her.

"Toban!" She ran to him, heedless of any dangers that might be lurking nearby, but when she got there a luminescent mist rose from the ground where Toban had been, and a white owl, no bigger than the size of her closed hand, rose into the air and disappeared into the forest.

Toban was gone.

"You didn't think it would be that easy, did you?"

Reiana whirled around, wobbling on unsteady feet, her heart racing. "Who are you?" she demanded, though she feared she recognised the voice. "Show yourself!"

A mocking laugh answered and from the shadows materialised a tall form. Gone was the hat, the dark cloak, the silk shirt, all semblance of a human. What stood before her now was an alien creature of primal beauty. A mane of white hair framed a feline face, crimson eyes stared malevolently at Reiana, and sharp teeth glinted in the pale moonlight. A skull adorned one shoulder like a pauldron above a bare chest of rippled muscle. Dark trousers were tucked into boots with more skulls at his knees, and a strange kilt, like a half-cape, was tucked around his waist under a belt of gold coins.

It was the Evay; she was sure of it. But rather than being a creature of light like the stories said, he dripped shadow.

"You."

"Yes, me," he agreed and moved toward her. She couldn't

be sure under the half-light of the moon, but it seemed to Reiana that the grass withered beneath his feet.

"You don't look like an Evay," Reiana said, backing away from the creature.

"Because I am not!" Rage twisted his face. "I," he continued, making an effort to control himself once more, "am Dasha'vay."

A voidsworn Evay! "Stay back!" Reiana said, raising her dagger like a sword.

"You can no more stop me than your grandmother could," the Dasha'vay said dismissively.

"Grandmother?" As much as she hated herself for asking, the words slipped from her tongue all the same. "Is she all right? What have you done with her?"

"I have done nothing," he said, though his face twisted strangely as though thinking of something unpleasant. He shook its head. "No. The question is, what has she done to you?"

Reiana frowned, her heart racing as memories of all that her grandmother had subjected her to over the years flashed through her mind. She pushed the thoughts away. "What? My grandmother has done nothing!"

"Nothing? Really? She set you chasing your cousin while the other children were sent to seek shelter."

"It was my task to look after Toban; Grandmother is too old to—" Reiana backed away, her dagger held tight. "What have you done with him?"

"I have done nothing," the Dasha'vay said. "The boy is with your grandmother as was always intended."

"You lie. I saw you take him!"

"A ruse to lead you here."

Reiana faltered. The Evay were tricksters, but the Dasha'vay were voidsworn. She could trust nothing from his mouth, but her grandmother had never been kind to her. Could this have all been an act? "Why?"

"Because you are to be given to the Shaluay," the Dasha'vay said. "Your grandmother made a bargain with *me*. I was to find bandits to attack your caravan and then lead you off after your precious cousin, lead you here."

"No, I don't believe you!" Reiana said.

"Why ever not? Is it because she has been such a kind and loving grandparent?" He eyed her, a crimson glow lighting his eyes in the dark. "There is something about you, child. Your grandmother has promised you to the Shaluay Starbinders. I don't know why, and I do not care. But none treat me as your grandmother has without retribution. She wants you to go to the Shaluay? I shall not allow it."

The Shaluay? What did he mean? Reiana opened her mouth to speak when a figure stepped out from behind the Dasha'vay. The night painted broad swathes of shadow across its features, but fair hair shone pale in the moonlight. It moved with a... a limp? The figure stepped into a moonbeam, and Reiana gasped, her blood freezing inside her veins. She knew that gait. The limp.

"Pr-Pren? Is that you? It's me. Reiana!"

"Whoever this was is long gone," the Dasha'vay said, teeth gleaming in a rictus grin. He gestured. "Take her."

"Stay back!" Reiana cried. She held her dagger out before her—the same dagger that Pren had crafted for her—fear tightening her throat. But the thing wearing Pren's body lurched forward. Even in the pale light of the moon, he looked washed out, leeched of colour. Of life. His gait, while never even, had always been smooth. But now, he moved as if he had forgotten how to walk entirely.

"No," she whispered, fear rooting her to the spot. "No. What's happened to you? Pren?"

The Dasha'vay laughed, a sound full of icy malice. "Your grandmother thinks she is very clever, and it's true that I cannot kill you, but I can make sure you don't get to the Starbinders like she wants. Give yourself to me."

A chittering growl rose in the dark, and Reiana realised that it was coming from Pren's mouth, his jaw slack and hanging open. In growing horror, she watched him lurch toward her, his arms outstretched, and his fingers twisted like claws.

"No!" Reiana screamed. She turned away from the ghul to flee, but it grabbed her shawl, pulling her back.

She spun around, her dagger slashing at the creature. Her arm felt weak, as if terror had drained all the strength from her, but the sharp steel connected with Pren's—no! It wasn't Pren—connected with the ghul's cheek, and it let out an unearthly scream before striking her with its other hand.

Stars exploded behind her left eye, her head rang.

"What did you do?" the Dasha'vay demanded. "Steel cannot hurt a ghul!

"Leave me alone!" Reiana cried, backing away, dagger gripped tight.

"*Asharak bhal tor!*" The Dasha'vay spat the words, and threads of violet smoke erupted from the ground all around Reiana. The smoke latched onto her, solidifying into delicate chains. They grasped her wrists, her arms, and legs, holding her firm. She struggled against them, terror rising as the thing, the ghul, came closer, black blood dripping from the cut she'd made and a horrifying chittering coming from its open mouth.

"Let me go!" She screamed, desperate to bring her dagger up, but the chains were as strong as those made by Korig, the clan's blacksmith.

"I don't believe I will," the Dasha'vay said as the ghul's hand—cold and hard—grasped her throat. "I will strip away every vein of whatever power is inside you and leave your husk for your wretched grandmother to spit on!"

Reiana thrashed against the ghul's icy grip. She wanted to wail in terror, but she could barely breathe. Still, a part of her searched Pren's face, seeking any part of him that might be left. His eyes, once blue and full of life, glowed with violet light. He'd been hurt in the fight against the bandits; she could see the dried blood on his chest and the cut across his torso that must have claimed his life...

Pren. Oh, Pren!

The howl that rose behind her lips was one of grief. Pren was dead. He'd died to protect the clan against the bandits.

Bandits her grandmother had hired? *If* that were true. If she could believe anything a voidspawn said.

Why was this happening? What had she ever done that this would be happening because of her? The Shaluay? What did they have to do with the clan, with her grandmother? What did they want with her?

"Scream all you want, poppet," the Dasha'vay said as he approached, his eyes flashing red. "No one will hear you out here."

"Help… me…" Reiana cried in desperation, barely able to form the words behind the ghul's grasp. She didn't know who she was calling to for help or how far from the camp she'd come chasing Toban, but she had to get away.

Reiana strained against the chains that held her arms. The ghul leant close, its mouth opening wide, and a black tongue darted out to lick her cheek. Fetid breath rolled over her, the stench of death and rot filling her nose. She twisted her head away, crying out.

She closed her eyes, unable to look at the dead face of the boy she had loved. Reiana could hear the footsteps of the Dasha'vay as he neared, and she strained with all her failing strength.

"Please!"

A single chime sounded at the back of her mind.

The topaz pendant at her neck flared to life. Light, brilliant, white, and pure, exploded into the night, and a chorus of crystalline chimes filled her ears.

The grave-cold hand grasping her throat fell away and the

ghul that wore Pren scrambled back as though the light was a wave of force pushing it from her. It snarled in anger, its face contorted in an inhuman expression of rage. Something within it surged forward, pushing against the light blazing from Reiana's pendant. The violet embers in its eyes blazed, burning like dark suns.

Reiana couldn't move. Power roared through her, an energy she'd never before known swelled in harmony with the chimes ringing in her ears.

She felt no heat from the light, but where it touched the ghul, it burned. The nauseatingly sweet stench of charred flesh filled Reiana's nose, and she tasted bile at the back of her throat. Oh, how she wanted to wretch, to fall to her knees gagging, but the power running through her held her upright, lifting her from the ground.

The violet light of the Void flared once more in the ghul's eyes before it winked out of existence. The sound of a scream fading into nothing filled the ruins as Pren's body collapsed, and Reiana felt her heels touch the earth once more before her legs buckled, and she fell to her knees.

The Dasha'vay screeched. "What have you done?"

Reiana blinked. She didn't know what she had done. *Oh, Pren. My love!*

The pendant at her neck was still alight, shining, and the chiming was still ringing in her ears but the tone, the song, was hard, rough, discordant.

The Dasha'vay stretched his hand toward her, his figure stark and pallid in the light, and he hissed guttural words

Reiana couldn't make out. More smokey chains burst from the ground only to dissipate as they touched the light of the pendant.

Reiana struggled to her feet. More of the ruins were revealed as the light fell on them. Tall columns and broken pillars reached for the heavens, some capped like grand archways, and in the night sky above them, five spheres of golden light, like bubbles of blown glass, rotated in a circle. They hadn't been there before, had they?

The Dasha'vay screeched again. Reiana backed away from the creature, stepping between two pillars that formed an archway behind her.

When the light from her pendant fell across the ground between the arches, the spheres above flashed with light and slowed their circling. The Dasha'vay looked up, eyes widening, and Reiana's eyes followed to see the spheres break from their pattern to float down toward her. They began to circle her as they came level, slowly weaving around her and shedding more light across the ruined complex.

"No. You will not escape me!"

The Dasha'vay stepped forward, shadows rising around it like a cloak, and the spheres flared like tiny suns and shot forward.

The Dasha'vay screamed again, this time in terror.

"She is not for you," said a disembodied voice. *"Come, Reiana. Come, child of the Stargazer. We await you."*

CHAPTER FIVE

REIANA STARED IN horror as the shadows around the voidsworn Evay were burnt away, and his skin began to melt beneath the light. Blood ran, flowing down his limbs. Bone emerged as his flesh dissolved, and his hair burst into flame. The Dasha'vay's scream became primal, a hapless call of horror so profound Reiana could feel it even after the spheres exploded in a soundless detonation. Reiana had to turn away from the sight.

A wall of force pushed her forward, and she stumbled, catching herself on one of the broken pillars. At her touch, runes around its base began to glow, and lines of light appeared across the paving stones, stretching into the ruins and illuminating the ancient complex before her.

The night fell back before the golden lines of light.

Reiana looked over her shoulder at the dark forest. She knew she should make her way back to the camp. To find Toban. But doing so would mean passing Pren's body, lying on the ground where he'd fallen, and she couldn't bring herself to do that. Tears burned her eyes. Not yet. And if what the Dasha'vay had said was true, her grandmother had sent her here to get rid of her. Could she even go back to the camp?

No. No, she wouldn't believe that. She *couldn't*.

And there was the voice that had called to her. Who was that?

Reiana took a breath, wiping the tears from her face.

She could feel the power of this ancient place stirring from a long slumber, and she turned her attention away from the lies of the Dasha'vay, away from Pren's body—she wanted to wail at the thought but pushed it down—instead, she tried to recall the stories she'd been told of the Shaluay. Of the great complexes that were places of healing and knowledge. Home to the Starwells, the fonts of Shaluay power in the world.

This place must have lain forgotten since the Sundering. So much had been lost to them. Mountains had moved, and seas had swallowed realms. Cities collapsed, and forests had burned and rivers had shifted course while new forests grew where none had been before.

She stepped forward, away from Pren, and made her way deeper into the ruins.

As she ventured in, more runes and geometric sigils ignited, revealing broken walls and leading Reiana down an arcade to a dais that held a dark, empty well.

Reiana stepped forward on trembling legs, up onto the platform that held the well.

The space before her was larger than the wells she was

used to. It was maybe sixteen feet across with a small wall of stone that came halfway up her shin, running around its edge, guarding the unwary against falling in.

Stopping just before the edge, Reiana peered into its dark depths and saw that the well wasn't empty at all.

It was filled with stars.

Every constellation of the heavens sat in its correct house and position, and as she watched they began to move, to spiral around a central axis.

The stars swelled up out of the confines of the well into a column of glittering pinpricks. Every star and constellation she had studied at her grandmother's feet was displayed in perfect detail, and behind those she recognised were hundreds, thousands more. It was *beautiful*.

As she stared, she realised she could no longer hear the chiming that had accompanied her so often that night. Reiana looked around. There was no sign of the Dasha'vay, not that she thought he might have survived whatever those globes of light had done, but there was no sign of Toban either.

Toban! How could she have forgotten him? She had *seen* the Dasha'vay take him from the camp, and she knew better than to trust the lies of a voidsworn Evay. Toban had to be here somewhere!

She spun around, but the lights that shone in the complex made the darkness outside all the more impenetrable. Reiana stepped away from the well. She didn't have time for this; she had to find her cousin.

"Toban is well, child."

Reiana gave a start. It was the same voice she'd heard in her mind earlier.

Slowly Reiana turned, searching the darkness for some possible source, her heart thundering in her chest like the pounding hooves of a hundred Dominarian horses in full charge.

"Don't be afraid, Reiana. I mean you no harm." The voice was male and sounded old.

"Who are you?" Reiana asked. Then shook her head. What was she doing? She had to find Toban.

"My name is Vendran," he said. *"As to where your cousin Toban is, fear not, he is safe."*

"I don't believe you!" Reiana said, fear lending her courage. "Where are you? Show yourself."

"I am not lying, child."

"Where is he? Where is Toban?"

"Come closer," Vendran said in her mind. *"Look in the well, and you will see."*

Reiana looked at the motes of light floating in the column before her. "All I see are stars."

"You must look in the well, Reiana."

She took a breath. Reiana didn't know where her hesitance was coming from, but something about this entire situation was… not right. Straightening, she stepped back to the edge of the well and looked down.

The light of the tiny stars floating within the well's boundaries did nothing to reveal the full reach of its depths; the darkness looked to go on forever. But as Reiana peered

Mark Timmony

down, the whirling spirals and brilliant nebulae began to converge, forming a bright circle of light and within its frame appeared the image of man. Clothed in black robes edged in silver, the man looked directly at her, his long hair pulled back from his lined face, his eyes a piercing blue, and in a silver torque at his neck shone an Amethyst stone, tinting his complexion and white hair with lilac fire.

He looked back at her as though he stood on the other side of an open doorway. "Hello, Reiana," the man said, his voice rough with age but strong still. "I am Vendran Sabay, Starmaster of the Shaluay Starbinders."

Reiana felt her mouth fall open. *Starmaster.* He was the most powerful Starbinder in all the realms. What was he doing here with her? She shook her head. It didn't matter. She had to find Toban!

"No, Reiana," Vendran said, again answering her thoughts. "Toban is not lost. He was never here."

Reiana frowned. "But I saw the Dasha'vay take him. That's why I followed him here."

"Yes," Vendran agreed. "You saw him take your cousin, but he did not bring him here. In that, the creature spoke truly."

"But I followed him the whole way," Reiana insisted. "He was only out of my sight for a few seconds."

"The Evay have a reputation as tricksters, but it is, in fact, their dark cousins, the Dasha'vay, to whom that reputation properly belongs," Vendran said, motes of light drifting across his image in the well. "After a few steps into the forest, the

75

Dasha'vay cast an illusion to hide himself and Toban. You chased a ghost owl he had bound to lead you here."

"Why?" Reiana felt a pit open in her stomach.

Vendran sighed, sorrow lining his face. "Let me show you."

The Starmaster's image faded, and stars filled the well once more. They began to move, rushing past her eyes, more and more points of light joining together until they began to form an image that resolved itself into the interior of her grandmother's caravan. Reiana lowered herself to her knees, looking over the rim of the well, and the image rushed forward until it seemed she was standing within it.

———·———

Relosa pressed her back to the caravan door. The screams outside still rose as those... *creatures* finished with one victim and moved on to the next.

She'd sensed the taint of *Des'maadr* as soon as the things had entered the Heartspace. The bandit attack had knocked over some of the torches that usually ringed the camp, leaving a gaping hole in the defences that most clansfolk didn't even know were there. Those defences—wards worked into the iron staves that held the torches— had protected all the clans of Nemisdrillion since the Sundering, creating a barrier that no Void-touched creature could penetrate. That the wards were still set at all was more habit than need these days. She should have been more careful dealing with that Dasha'vay! She had bargained only for the protection of Toban and

Reiana, and never contemplated for a second that its malice would lead it to attack the clan when she'd removed it from her caravan.

Stupid, stupid woman!

"Grandmother?"

"Toban, dear child!" Relosa pushed herself from the door and hurried to the bed.

"What's happening, Grandmother?" Toban asked, a tremor in his voice, as she swept him up into her arms.

"Shhh, child, don't be scared. You are safe here," she told him. He squirmed in her embrace, but she couldn't let him go.

"There was a man," Toban said. "He took me."

"Hush, it was just a bad dream."

Toban managed to push himself back so he could look at her face. "It wasn't a dream, Grandmother. Reiana was there too. Where is she?"

Relosa felt her face twist as grief welled up at the mention of her granddaughter, but Toban misunderstood.

"Don't be angry with Reiana, Grandmother!" He took on an expression far too serious for his years. "She tried to save me. She's always looked after me."

"I'm not angry with her," Relosa said.

"Yes, you are. You're always mean to her. She's a good girl."

Relosa's heart twisted at his words. Gods above, what had she done to the girl? But she couldn't answer him. She couldn't speak. Years of conditioning herself against praising Reiana, of showing her any kindness, affection, *love*, still bound her like iron chains.

Outside the caravan came a shout, followed by a high-pitched whine, almost a scream.

Toban shifted in her arms, looking toward the shuttered windows. "What was that?"

"I don't know." A fierce banging came at the door, and her heart leapt to her throat. If it was another clan member begging to be let in—

"Mother! Mother are you there?"

"Jaril! Thank the stars!" Relosa said at the same time as Toban jumped up from her arms.

"Papa!" he cried and made for the door, but Relosa grabbed his arm and hauled him

back.

"No," she hissed. "Wait. I will check."

Toban frowned. "Do you think it's the bad man?"

Relosa froze. The bad man? Who did he—the banging came again.

"Mother!"

"Wait!" she told Toban and made her way to the door. Taking a breath, she opened a small square window and peered out. It was dark beyond, but she could see the man before her door clearly. Tall and dark-haired, he looked more like his father every year as his beard began to show streaks of grey. His eyes were shadowed, and he held his sword in his hand, its length still dark with blood, his leather armour was stained with it too, but she recognised her son. Behind him, more of the clansfolk who had gone hunting were helping those who had remained to drag the long, white, glistening bodies of five creatures to the fire at the centre of the Heartspace.

"What are those idiots doing?" she demanded. "Those creatures need to be put outside the bounds of the wards!"

"Let me in, Mother. Where is Toban?"

"I'm here, Papa!" Toban had run up beside her.

Relosa pulled back the bolt to let Jaril in.

"Papa!" Toban pushed the door open to be swept up in his father's arms as Jaril bounded up the short steps. "What happened?"

"I don't know, Son," Jaril said, putting Toban down. He made to hug Relosa, but she waved him away.

"You're covered in filth," she said, indicating his leather.

Jaril grunted. "When we returned, those things were in the camp. But there were bodies outside the circle as well as in the Heartspace. I cut the one on Karin in half, but she," he shook his head. "She was already gone. It looked like it sucked all the blood from her. Those things are borewyrms, Mother. Young, but still borewyrms. We are leagues away from the Borderlands. What are they doing here?" He slapped his hand against the doorframe, shaking his head. "I can't make out what happened. Seven of the clansfolk we left behind are dead. Borewyrms are daemonspawn! How'd they get in?"

"We were attacked," Relosa said, moving to the now-covered table. She sat before her trembling legs gave out beneath her. "Bandits attacked us at dusk. Karin and the others fought them off, but they must have knocked over the torch posts, ruining the wards. It would only take one out of place to make the circle useless."

"Did you see Reiana, Papa?" Toban asked, grabbing his father's hand.

"She's not here?" Jaril looked at Relosa, and it took all her strength not to flinch at the accusation in his eyes.

"No," Toban said, shaking his head. "She tried to save me from the strange man. She ran after him when he took me."

"No!" Relosa straightened as the shout left her mouth. "Toban," she said, moderating her tone, "that was just a bad dream."

Toban shook his head. "It wasn't! You talked to him when he brought me back. When his eyes went all red—"

"Toban, stop telling tales!"

"I'm not!" Toban's face took on a stubborn cast. "He told you he had done what you'd asked!"

"Mother?" Jaril's voice was low.

"What?" she demanded. "He's been asleep. How could he—"

"Toban's not a liar. And you have never treated that girl properly! What have you done?"

Bah! She didn't need this now. She was the one who'd had to make the decisions, who had pushed Reiana away. Not him, not any of them! "I did what needed to be done. She couldn't stay here."

"Couldn't stay here? We are her *family*. She was Iane's only child. All we had left of your daughter, my *sister*. I should have taken her in myself—"

"Ha! You were too busy leading the clan and looking after your own family!"

Jaril opened his mouth to speak, rage colouring his face, but he closed his eyes and took a deep breath. "So, this is all your doing? The dead outside? The borewyrms?"

"No!" She pushed out of the chair.

"Void take you, *yes*!" Jaril barked. "All your secrets and mysteries. This is exactly what you'd do. Tell me, what have you done with Reiana?"

"She is gone," Relosa snapped. "And good riddance!" The words were out of her mouth by force of habit before she could stop them, and she couldn't call them back.

"Mother!" Jaril stared at her in shock. "What happened to you after Iane's death? It was not Reiana's fault! What turned you so heartless to a child of your own flesh and blood?"

Relosa couldn't answer him. She'd built the illusion that she cared naught for her granddaughter for over fifteen years; she couldn't let it go until Reiana was well and truly amongst the Shaluay, no matter how it writhed within her.

Once Reiana was amongst the Starbinders, there would be no chance of turning back For Reiana or herself, but she'd accepted her role long ago.

Jaril shook his head in disgust at her silence.

"She's gone to the Starwell, Papa," Toban said.

"Toban!" Relosa felt icy fingers wrap around her throat.

"The Starwell?" Jaril said. "It's nothing but a bunch of ruins."

"That's where the bad man said he was leading Reiana," Toban said.

"Good boy, Toban." Jaril knelt on one knee to look his son in the eye. "You stay here. I don't want you going out tonight until your ma or I are back. Your grandmother's caravan is safest. You hear me?"

"Yes, Papa." Toban nodded.

"I will be back," Jaril said, rising to his feet. "What you have done tonight is unforgivable." He raised his hand to head. "You are just like your own mother. All the secrets, all the lies, thinking you know better than everyone else. Her secrets killed my grandfather, your father. The Old World is gone, Mother. It is no more, thanks to the Summoners, and your precious Shaluay did not save us. Do not speak!" He cut the air with a slashing motion as Relosa opened her mouth. "You will explain yourself to the elders, and to me, when I return."

With that, Jaril stormed out of the caravan, slamming the door behind him. Relosa heard him call for Garna and Dane, his closest friends and the best warriors amongst the clan.

Relosa couldn't speak, her throat was tight, and tears blurred her sight. He wouldn't save Reiana. He couldn't. Stars help her. He *mustn't* get there in time. Reiana had to be taken by the Shaluay. She had to!

"Don't cry, Grandmother." A small hand reached up to pat her shoulder. "Papa will find Reiana."

Wordlessly, Relosa gathered Toban in her arms and wept.

———•———

Reiana came back to herself as the scene faded. In the Starwell the image of Vendran—the Starmaster, she corrected herself— reformed itself out of a web of starlight, but she found it difficult to focus. Her chest felt like bands of iron were tightening around it, and she had to force herself to breathe.

"She is gone. And good riddance!"

Her grandmother's words rang in her mind.

Grandmother had been the one who had set her on this path. Her grandmother had sent her after Toban, knowing full well that he was safe and that Reiana would be led by a Dasha'vay to this place. She had called the creature that had caused the deaths of so many of the clan. Had turned Pren into—no! She shut that thought from her mind.

Why? Did her grandmother hate her that much? What had she ever done but been born?

No child could be blamed for their mother dying in childbirth.

A splash on her hand startled her, and she looked down to see her mother's pendant, the topaz stone that had lit her path tonight. Another drop splashed on her closed fist. Tears.

Her grandmother had wanted her to come here and had gone to extraordinary lengths to achieve it. Reiana wondered what her fate would have been if the defences of the Starwell had not activated for her. The stories of what the Dasha'vay did with their prey were rarely told around the campfires.

"She is gone. And good riddance!"

Reiana raised her hands to face, sobbing. Pain wracked her body as though each cry was wrenched from her soul. Thoughts of her grandmother's betrayal, the years of cruelty, blazed like fire in her heart.

"It hurts now, child, I know, but one day you will understand the sacrifice your grandmother has made to bring you here," Vendran said, but Reiana took no comfort from his words. "We cannot fully know the path the stars lay before us. They have already moved on before the light of their passing reaches us. We dance to their song, it is true, but their path is no secret tyranny. Their movement creates tides, the currents that push and pull the knowing and unknowing. Come to me, child, come to the Shaluay. From us, you will learn to see those tides, to navigate those currents, and never be at their mercy unwittingly again."

Reiana gazed into the shifting, glittering stars of the well. "But if the path has already been set, we cannot change it," she said, her voice hoarse.

"No, we cannot change what has happened," Vendran agreed, "but knowledge, understanding of it and what comes next allows us to plan our response, to choose which way we will move forward. Our actions lead us to branches in the road, ways we had not considered, and so we gain the chance to affect how we receive it."

"No choice can bring Pren back to me," she said, wiping her eyes.

"No, Reiana, it cannot. We cannot call a soul back once it passes Samantra's Veil. That is the way of *Des'maadr*, and what power the Shaluay have does not touch that of the Void."

"Then what use are you to me?" Reiana snapped, anger welling inside her. "I have lost everything, my family, my love. My future…"

"Only the future you thought you had," Vendran sighed. "It is small comfort I know, but the world lies before you still. This pain will pass. Come to me, Reiana, come to Arleth'taur. There is a new home waiting for you. New brothers and sisters to support you."

Reiana stared at the Starmaster, stared at this image floating amongst a sea of stars. "Come to you?"

"You need never be lost or lonely again. You have the gift, child, and the Shaluay shall teach you all you need to know. You hear the call of the stars," the Starmaster's eyes were bright pinpricks regarding her. "Follow them. Follow the stars and come home."

Reiana choked back her tears. Home. She'd had a home amongst the clan once. Now this stranger offered her another. A different choice. A better choice? Reiana had spent years at her grandmother's side, learning the wisdom passed down through their bloodline. That had been her place, that had been her *home*. But she had been discarded, people killed, all because the stars had different plans for her? The pain thrumming in her core stilled. A white noise, a voiceless hiss, fell over her ears and then faded away, taking with it all her confusion and heartache.

Come home.

"Pren?"

Reiana got to her feet.

All she had ever wanted for so long was to belong. To be loved. She had tried to love her grandmother, tried to be what she had thought the woman wanted her to be, but it had never been enough. Reiana had found love with Pren but that too had been taken away by the same person who had pushed her here. Forced her into exile.

She examined her heart and found she no longer cared.

Her thoughts turned to Toban, but he was loved. He was cherished. He'd be fine.

She felt light. Weightless.

She wanted to laugh.

Was this what it felt like to be at peace?

Reiana was tired. So very tired. She wanted to sleep, to close her eyes and never have to wake.

"Yes," she whispered. *To sleep.*

"Come to Arleth'taur, Reiana, and let me teach you. I shall open a path—"

"No," Reiana said and stepped up onto the edge of the Starwell. "If the stars have written such a path for me as the one I have walked, then I don't think I want to serve them. You say the stars are not tyrannous, but they are certainly unfair."

Clasping her mother's pendant, she pulled down hard, breaking the chain. This stone was said to be a gift of the

Shaluay, a token of the stars. She didn't need it anymore, and she certainly didn't want it. She opened her hand and let it fall. The stone tinkled as it hit the platform, but she didn't see where it went.

She stepped up onto the wall around the well and glanced down. The open mouth of the Starwell was dark; even with the stars that glittered like chips of ice in its depths, she could not make out the bottom. It was an emptiness that went on forever.

"I have had enough of cruelty," she said. *Pren, I'm coming.*

Reiana stepped off the ledge.

Jaril, Garna and Dane exited the forest at a run. They'd had to leave the horses at the camp, much to Jaril's disgust, but there was no trail through the woods that the animals could easily navigate in the dark.

One of the clan's tracking dogs pulled on the lead that Garna held, the shorter, thickly built man holding the big hound steady as it strained forward. The dog had Rei's scent and had led them unfalteringly through the forest.

Beside them, Dane held a lantern aloft, the yellow light shining on his black skin. Tall and lean, Dane's other hand was wrapped firmly around the hilt of his sword as he scanned the ground down the slope of the hill before them and to the trees beyond.

"She can't have gone much farther, surely?" Dane's voice was a deep bass in the dark.

"We'll know when we find her." Jaril peered ahead, trying to see through the dark mass of forest that rose again across the small stream at the base of the hill. "Did you see that?"

"See what?" Dane said.

"A light." Jaril pointed. "Through the trees."

"There are no townsfolk out this way," Dane said. "Not this close to what's left of the Atresian Plains."

"It wasn't the yellow of firelight," Jaril said. "It was white."

"White?" Garna spat to the side. "Never heard of a white light before, 'least not outside of a Shrine. Don't see it here neither, but Jax here is keen to get to sumthin'."

"Void take it! Where is she?"

"Can't blame yourself, Jar," Dane said beside him.

"Then who do I blame?"

"Are you an Elder God now? Or one of those, what do they call them, Sholmen?"

"Shol'mas," Garna corrected. "Divine messengers, or so they say."

"Right." Dane nodded. "Shol'mas. You couldn't have known the camp would be attacked."

"You're taking too much on yourself, my friend," Garna added. "You're a good leader, but you can't predict everything

Jaril clenched his jaw to keep from speaking. If this had been a normal attack, villagers or city folk running them off, then his friends would be correct. But this was the result of his mother and her crazy hatred of Reiana. It wasn't the girl's fault her mother had died in childbirth! He should have done something sooner, taken Rei into his own caravan to raise. Teala would have welcomed her. But he was too busy looking after everyone else, so he'd left his niece with his mother, who'd—

A pillar of brilliant white light shot into the sky from half a mile away. The trees before them were clearly revealed as though it were daylight.

Jax began barking wildly, and Garna struggled to hold the hound as he pulled on the leash.

"What in the name of the Elder…" Dane trailed off, the light from his lantern now a candle beside a bonfire.

"She's that way. Come on!" Jaril set off at a run, trusting his friends to follow. What had his mother done?

CHAPTER SIX

VENDRAN STAGGERED BACK from the Starwell, a wave of light and sound erupting in a column of energy as Reiana fell into the open vortex of the well on the other side of the continent.

Idiot! I should have seen this was too much for her.

But he hadn't seen it. The Probability Matrix had not accounted for such a choice. What had changed? What variable in her profile had not been taken into consideration?

He had no time!

"What happened?" Arais was beside him.

"She has stepped into the well."

"But—"

"I know!" He took a breath; he needed a clear mind. This was too important for him to fail. The future of the Shaluay and the world rested on that girl.

Red sigils were flashing in warning on the console.

"Do what you can to stabilise the Astra field. I will open the Path,"Vendran said.

"There isn't enough power in the wells to achieve an active Path,"Arais protested as she turned her attention to the Altar, her fingers touching sigils and drawing new ones on the crystal surface.

"There is enough power in this well, and I can provide the rest to the Starwell Reiana jumped into."

"You'll drain your cora'stone!"

"It is worth the risk. *She* is worth the risk,"Vendran said.

"But the consequences. You'll d—"

"I am aware!" His life was nothing compared to hers. To what she would become. It was worth the risk. It had to be. "She was wearing a naru'stone. Look for its imprint on her aura," he said and then closed his eyes, blocking everything else out.

Centring his thoughts with the ease of long practise, Vendran shifted his consciousness into the cora'stone at his neck. Fractals and lines of geometric light surrounded him as he sank within the stone's depths. Linked glowing sigils formed lines like script, and he swiped them with an ethereal hand. The sigils spread at the gesture like a deck of cards dealt across a table, hanging in the space before his perception. Sigils of power, wards of protection, binding, and funnels that shaped and mastered energy; and behind them, deeper still were the high sigils that shuttered the power of his Amethyst cora'stone. He lowered those high wards with a flick of his mind and merged with that now unfettered power. Pausing, he oriented himself and then cast his awareness into the centre of the Starwell.

White light filled his perceptions as he followed the thread back to the well at the sixty-eighth complex. But he knew how to navigate the forces the Shaluay had bound together when humanity first arrived on Sobia nearly twenty millennia ago. The first Shaluay, an Order long before there were Summoners, had used the old Tek of Erth to build the bases that would lead humanity out of the darkness they had fallen into. But things had not followed the path those masters had predicted, and the discovery of *Asai* had sent the world in a different direction. But the Shaluay endured. To guide and protect, to heal and to shelter. The ancient knowledge had been integrated into the new ways, and as Starmaster of the Shaluay, he knew them all.

He spun his awareness through the buffeting stellar winds that quantum manipulation had bound in the Astra fields of the wells, looking for the single spark that was the imprint of the naru'stone Reiana had worn at her neck. He channelled more of the power held within his cora'stone. Vendran removed the final buffers placed around that power and let it pour through him. Fire burned along his veins, his aged bones glowing molten beneath his skin. He blocked the pain, ignored it with a will whose strength had been honed over centuries. The air in his lungs burned, and he knew he was dying, that the power was killing him, that he was allowing it to kill him. But his life was worth the sacrifice. For her. For the girl who would find an Empyros.

With a last gasp, he *reached*.

———•———

An explosion of light blinded Reiana as she dropped into the well. Adrenaline exploded in her veins, a surge of sensation that overwhelmed the feeling that she'd left her stomach somewhere behind her. Wind rose from the depths, buffeting her and slowing her descent as the chiming she had been hearing all night returned, rising to such a screaming pitch it almost rendered her senseless.

She was falling, she knew that; the stars of the well were gone, so she must have fallen past them, and with no light, she could see nothing before her. Even with her arms outstretched, Reiana could feel nothing around her.

The longer she fell without landing, the greater the fear inside her grew. What had she done?

The fog that had clouded her mind was gone, and she began to scream, the wind blasting into her open mouth like the fiercest storm. She fumbled at her throat, seeking the only piece of her mother she had left, and her heart wrenched as she remembered yanking it from her neck.

She cried, but the winds dried her tears before they fell.

Mother, help me!

She knew her plea was useless. The dead that passed Samantra's Veil did not reply to those they left behind. She was cold. Her limbs aching as though she was outdoors in the dead of winter. Around her, Reiana noticed a blue light lining her body, sparkling like hoarfrost, and pale blue flames whipped over her extremities like a fire caught in a breeze.

It was as though she'd fallen through a hole in the world. A brief terror that she'd fallen into the Void itself flashed through her thoughts but was just as swiftly gone. Reiana struggled against the lethargy overcoming her, stretched her mind and awareness out into the great darkness. She didn't want to die. She shouldn't have jumped.

Mother. Please.

She reached her senses out and brushed against… something.

Her mind jerked to alertness, though it was not a physical presence she felt.

She searched again, stretching her mind like she would her arm.

And there she found it. Insubstantial, like a wisp or a dream, it was a presence that she could just make out.

A form built of starlight, a constellation so vast it suddenly loomed around her and outstretched the limits of her comprehension.

She felt its notice, its neutral regard, like the attention she might offer an ant.

And she felt that notice sharpen, focus on her as stars suddenly blazed around her and white light slammed around her falling body, and her mind fell into darkness.

———·—

Vendran's spirit soared on the Astra fields connecting the Starwells. He knew his body had collapsed in Arleth'taur. That even now, Arais was stretching her own abilities to stabilise the Path he'd given his life to open.

His spirit sped across twelve hundred miles in the blink of an eye and dove down into the depths of the ruined well. As pure spirit, the formless Astra fields were revealed to him as a shifting mass of energies, undulating like the Borealis of the far south. It was a display that never ceased to impress him with its beauty, but there was no time to admire it now. Vendran gathered the power of his cora'stone around him, charging sigils of seeking and scripts of locating into ethereal nets that he cast before himself.

He had to find her. His power was not infinite, and already it was being used at a prodigious rate. Around him, the energies of the Starwell shifted and darkened, becoming an ocean of shadows that passed him in flickering images bled of colour like the designs of the Probability Matrix. He strained his senses, seeking the yellow glow of the naru'stone as it sank into the event horizon of the vortex of the well. Silhouettes of his past flashed by, images to distract his conscious mind, to separate the wheat from the chaff of those who would dare to impose their will on the primal matter of creation. Humankind was not built to play with the stuff of life, as the disaster wrought by the Summoners proved. But the Shaluay did not seek to control; they sought to guide. Theirs was not the imposition of control, of mastery, but the subtlety of persuasion and the cunning of coercion.

And those very forces rose around him to block his progress. The whispers of suggestion, the light touch that shifted the gaze, the distortion of reflections plied him with feather-soft caresses, and his trained mind ignored them all.

He continued to sink through the layers of vibration that formed the fabric of reality, and in the distance, he saw it. The cinder-like glow of the imprint Reiana's naru'stone left on her aura. Like the cora'stones the Shaluay worked with, the naru'stones were crafted in the vaults of Arleth'taur specifically to mould and guide accommodating minds toward melding with a cora'stone proper. A tool given to initiates of the Order and to those agents who worked on behalf of the Shaluay. Agents such as Reiana's grandmother.

Like an archer sighting his mark, Vendran aimed his awareness on the girl and—

He was brought up short with slamming force as stars formed the outline of a great cat, a panthress of the heavens, barring his way.

"Why do you seek the girl, servant of Sharné?"

He gazed at the Guardian of the Moon Goddess, Samantra, despair wrenching at his heart. He had no time. The energy he was using was almost gone.

"Great One, she is needed; she will lead an Empyros—"

"Does your world need one who can bind the Empyreans

again? Surely the damage your Summoners have caused is enough already. I am of a mind to grant the child the peace for which she so longs, having been victim to misguided prophecy already in her short life."

"Without an Empyros to stop them, the Des'maadrians will gain a foothold on Sobia. Even the Ancients would seek to stop such an event."

"Speak not to me, Son of Erth, of what the i'Malisantians would do or seek. It was the folly of the i'Mal that led to your dealings with Des'maadr."

"Please, Great One." He was not used to begging; his position never required it, but he was running out of time. "The Shaluay do not seek the glories of *Asai*; we do not interfere with the powers of creation—"

"Think you not? Asai is in all things, human, split your atoms, and you are touching the foundations of the universe itself though you are blind to it."

Vendran made to respond, but his mind faltered, the energy projecting his spirit-form dying as the power in his cora'stone flickered.

The Guardian of the Elder Goddess of the Moon roared, and a white light flared around him, his spirit stabilising.

"You stand at Samantra's Veil, human. Will you pass over? I can send you back from whence you came though it would not be a blessing given the damage you have done to your mortal form."

"No," Vendran begged. "Guardian, please. Save the girl; she is needed!"

"And so great is the need that you sacrifice your life for it?" The Guardian paused as though weighing Vendran's words against calculations he couldn't begin to fathom.

"The Veil of Manifestation is still torn on your world, and the threat of the Void to this universe is still of concern," the panthress said at last. *"Very well. Though the Elders remain neutral in all things, my mistress will allow this. I shall deliver the girl where you cannot, but you will not be there to train her. Do you trust the ones who will do so in your place?"*

Vendran felt such relief plunge through him that his mind spun. It took him precious moments to formulate a reply, though the Guardian seemed infinitely patient. What had she said? Did he trust the Collective? It was all he had left. The Starbinders that remained had the knowledge and ability to train new initiates, and his own knowledge came from the Shal'ashay itself. Any First Binder with the appropriate fortitude could delve the knowledge of the Starmasters from it.

A vision of Arais and the look that had flashed across her face when he had proclaimed Reiana to be the future of the Order rose in his mind. But there was no other way.

"Yes! Yes, Great One. Please save her."

"Very well. May the Light of the Eye guide you, Starmaster."

But he could not go without leaving Reiana some word, some understanding of what was ahead of her. He crafted a binding with his last breath and thrust it into the heart of his cora'stone back in Arleth'taur. It was a memory, a thought, a sending, tied to the vibration that was unique to Reiana. He prayed to the Elder Gods that she would find it; it was all that he could do.

The white light that had steadied him as the energy in his cora'stone failed, grew bright around him, blinding his senses and washing his thoughts until nothing remained.

The column of light blazing into the heavens disappeared just as the men reached a ruined compound. The sudden darkness blinded them, and Jaril stumbled, tripping over something on the ground.

He went sprawling forward, knocking the wind out of himself and lay gasping on the ground as Dane came forward with his lantern.

"Jaril," Dane said. "Take a look at this."

"That's another one then," Garna said, holding Jax close as the dog let out a whine, sniffing and snorting at something.

Jaril climbed to his feet. Part of him noted the tall, broken pillars around them as he turned back to Dane, but his blood froze as he saw the shadow of the body lying on the ground. The body he'd tripped over.

For a panicked moment, he thought they'd found Reiana, his skin pebbling as his stomach roiled. But his eyes adjusted, and the light of the lantern fell across a man's face, a boy's face really. The shadow of his first beard was still a pale imitation of what it might become. Would have become.

"Pren," Jaril said. Swallowing, he crouched over the young

man who'd been sweet on Reiana and laid two fingers on his neck. He was dead.

"What happened to him?" Garna said as Jax whined again and then sat at his side.

Jaril looked the young man over. His face was unblemished but for a cut at the top of his right cheek but his body… His tunic was ragged and what looked like a poorly healed incision ran from his collarbone to his waist, lying dark on his pale skin. That was new. What had his mother unleashed?

"I don't know," he said at last. He passed his hand over Pren's eyes to close them. "We need to find Reiana. If Pren is here, she can't be far."

"I don't know," Dane said. "What was that light? And what is this place?"

"It's old," Garna said. "Pre-Sundering if I was to guess."

"Summoner made?" Dane asked.

"No," Jaril snapped. "Shaluay."

"Oh," Garna said. "Well, that's all right then, ain't it? The Shaluay were allies of Nemisdrillion."

Dane grunted. "They can't have been that good if Pren is dead. The stories of the Starbinders are easily as strange as those of the Summoners. And who knows what they had guarding their—what'd they call them? Starpools?"

"Starwells," Jaril said, turning away from Pren to look around them.

"Aye," Dane agreed. "That's it. Starwells."

Jaril started forward. "This way."

The stone they walked over was still smooth, polished, but cracked in places, weeds growing in dark clumps and the surface made uneven by sunken flagstones and displaced pillars that had fallen across the walkway. He kept moving, the stars in the night sky clear and sparkling, taunting him as they made their way into the Shaluay complex, finally coming to a wide space that seemed to have been spared any of the ravages that blemished the ruins at their backs.

In front of Jaril was the wide circular dais that would hold the Starwell.

"Reiana!" He called into the still night. "Reiana!"

Garna came up beside him, Jax reluctant and dragging at his leash.

"Something strange here," Garna said. "No animals around tonight. And Jax don't want to be here."

"There'd been no animals around because of the daemons," Dane offered. "Those borewyrms at the camp would have sent all wildlife into hiding for miles around."

"Might wanna come back in daylight, Jaril," Garna said. "If she were here, she'd have answered."

Jaril was only half-listening; he was busy keeping his words behind his teeth. As Dane shifted beside him, the man moved his lantern, and Jaril saw a flash of light sparkle on the ground by the well.

"Dane," he said and reached out. "The lantern."

His friend passed it over without a word, and Jaril lowered the light, shining it across the floor in front of him. There, on the white stone, was a topaz gem on a silver chain. He picked it up, the chain cold against his hand. It was his sister Iane's necklace, the one Jaril had given to Reiana when she'd turned five, a keepsake of the mother she'd never had the chance to know. A necklace Reiana had never taken off.

The lantern fell from his other hand, a sharp crack coming from one of its glass panes, and he dropped to his knees, clutching the pendant to his chest. "Reiana!"

"What is it, Jar?" Dane said. "Where is she?"

Jaril closed his eyes against the heaving emotions in his chest, pushing them down into a tight ball of cold anger. "She's gone."

"Did she…" He heard Garna approach the edge of the well and opened his eyes to see the stocky man carefully leaning over the hole, Jax sniffing around the edge. "Did she fall?"

"I don't know," Jaril said.

"You can't know she's gone, Jar," Dane said. "We should wait for daylight and get more of the clan here to help."

"She's gone," Jaril said, thrusting his closed fist at Dane, the pendant dangling on its silver chain.

"Is that hers?"

"Yes, it was her mother's. Reiana has never taken it off since I gave it to her."

"Well, still…" Dane trailed off.

"We've lost a lot of people tonight," Garna said, his voice thick. "Pren, Reiana. Tora and Karin, and the others. Borewyrms." He shook his head. "If we could camp behind walls, this wouldn't happen."

"Ha!" Dane scoffed. "We wander, Garna. That's why we're called 'Wanderers'."

Jaril stood. "You're right, Garna, we've lost too many people over too many years. We used to have twenty caravans in the clan now we're down to twelve. Our wandering is over."

"The citadels?" Dane asked.

"Yes."

"I don't know what the elders or the rest of the clan will think of this plan," Garna said. "The citadels were built by the Summoners."

"And are still standing five hundred years after the Sundering," Jaril said. "No-one wants them and we can find safety there."

"Safety?" Dane asked. "So close to the Deadlands?"

"No more bandits, no more being chased from towns and villages. We will have our own place with walls to ward off any daemons who might attack us."

"And how will you convince your mother?" Garna shook his head. "Relosa is the one the elders will follow, and she holds on to the old ways."

Jaril felt his jaw tighten at mention of his mother. She would agree to this or he'd abandon her to the wolves after what she'd done this night. "You leave her to me."

—————

The first thing Reiana noticed was the lack of wind.

The second was that she was no longer moving.

She opened her eyes, blinking as she took in a strange room, a room bigger than anything she'd ever experienced amongst the caravans of the clan.

The ceiling soared above her, arching into darkness. At regular intervals on the curved walls around her were lamps—no, not lamps, stones?—that glowed with a soft white light very different to torchlight, and flickering in the centre of the room was a column of stars like the ones in the Starwell.

Where was she?

The floor she was lying on was made of metal that was cold under her hands. She pushed herself up and looked around. Beside her, on the floor, was an old man in dark robes, motionless.

Dead.

She'd seen enough death assisting her grandmother that she could recognise the signs. The movement of a chest as the lungs worked beneath it was never something you consciously noticed unless a person was gasping for breath, but when the lungs were not moving at all it was instantly apparent.

Bent over him was a woman in silver robes; long white hair veiled her face from Reiana's eyes, but she could hear her clearly.

"You old fool," the woman said to the man she knelt over. "Without a successor in place, you gave your life for this girl. And for what? *Why?*"

Reiana swallowed. That was Vendran on the floor. The Starmaster of the Shaluay. She knew it. And he… he was dead because of her.

A strange metallic noise and the thump of heavy steps behind her made Reiana gasp, and she twisted around.

She was on a long walkway that stretched back to a shadowed doorway. Approaching her was a humanoid figure of shining metal and glowing crystal. It looked like a suit of crystal armour, with joints of light and bands of energy running inside it like blood in veins.

A flare of panic gripped her as the walking suit of crystal and metal continued to approach, but it stopped five feet away in the centre of the walkway. Reiana scrambled to her feet; her hand dropped to her belt, but the dagger she'd used at the well was gone.

"The Starmaster is dead."

The words came from the woman behind her, and Reiana looked back over her shoulder. The woman lifted her head, and Reiana stared as blue skin was revealed. The woman was an Amarian. Reiana had never met an Amarian before, but she had heard tales of the haughty, arrogant natives of the realm the Sundering had turned into a desert.

"I must inform the Seneschal and initiate the early rousing protocols for the Collective." The woman reached over and took a clear quartz-like stone from the torque at the Starmaster's neck before rising to her feet. "All of that power, that knowledge, lost." She shook her head and finally looked at Reiana. "I hope you were worth it, child."

"I don't… What happened?"

"Vendran na'Sabay, the Starmaster of the Order of the

Shaluay Starbinders, saved you when you jumped into an open Astra field before it was connected to a Path."

"Why? Why am I worth saving? Even my grandmother didn't want me."

The woman tsked. "So young. Learn to look beyond yourself if you want answers, child. Your worth was valued so highly by the Starmaster that he died to save you from yourself. Try to be worthy of that legacy."

He'd died to save her.

Guilt and shame washed over Reiana. She had been so foolish! She had jumped into the Starwell in the forest thinking to escape, to die. And the Starmaster had to give his life to save her.

"I am Arais Sometsu. A Senior Binder of the Order," the Amarian said, her silver eyes staring inscrutably at Reiana. "What is your name, child?"

Reiana opened her mouth, then paused. "Iana," she said at last. "Iana Sabay."

Arais arched an eyebrow at this, but Iana held the woman's gaze. If this man had valued her so much that he would give his life to save hers, then she would honour his sacrifice, even if she didn't understand it. And she would take no part of her grandmother with her into this new life.

"Very well," Arais said at last. She held up the crystal she had taken from Vendran's neck. "This is a cora'stone, the basis of the Shaluay's power. Vendran had raised it to a tier-three ranked Amethyst. It is now blank. Tradition amongst the

Shaluay holds that a benefactor's cora'stone be passed on
to their student. Had he lived, I believe Vendran would have
taught you himself."

"Taught me?" Iana blinked, studying the inert cora'stone.
It was not smooth as she'd initially thought but intricately
faceted. "I am to be a Starbinder?"

"If you pass the Pairing of the Stone." A look Iana couldn't
make out flashed across Arais' face but was gone almost as
quickly as it appeared. The Senior Binder eyed the cora'stone
and then tossed it over.

Iana fumbled but managed to catch it before it fell.

As her hand closed around the cora'stone, her world
exploded into an ocean of stars.

Iana felt as though she were falling again, as though she
was back in the Starwell. Stars spun around her, twisting and
swirling and condensing to form an image of Vendran as he'd
appeared to her before.

*"Child, I have passed beyond Samantra's Veil long before I
planned and before I had a chance to explain to you why you
are here.*

*"You come from a long line of Stargazers through your
mother's family, though your grandmother failed to reveal
that in her grief at the knowledge that you had been chosen
to leave her and join us. With the Sundering caused by the
Summoners, our Order has declined, and that must be reversed.
The Starscroll Prophecies warn us that an Empyros will rise
when the Daemon Queen and her hordes return, but they
will have none to guide them with the Summoners gone. The*

Ciralys become more twisted with envy that the Summoners'
might is denied them each day and would prove poor teachers
to an Empyros—if any Summoner was allowed to live to reach
their potential. But the Shaluay can guide them.

"We must *guide them if we are to save any spark of*
humanity when the Daemon Queen comes again. And to do
that, we need one who can ascend to the rank of Starmaster
and lead us back to what we lost during the Sundering. You,
Reiana of the Wanderers, have been marked by Sharné. You
have the blood of Stargazers in your veins.

"Save the Shaluay, child, and save the world."

And just as quickly as the vision had come, Iana found
herself released, her mind reeling.

Lead the Shaluay? Teach an Empyros? A *Summoner*? How
could she do any of that?

If the stars believe in you, child, how can you not?

The voice sounded like the Starmaster's, and Iana looked
around, but no one was there.

"Come," Arais said, interrupting her thoughts.

Iana watched as the woman stepped around Vendran's
body and the strange automaton lumbered forward to pick
up the dead Starmaster. The man who'd seemed so vibrant in
her mind now looked shrunken and frail in the crystal arms
that carried him.

Something stirred in Iana as she considered all that had
just happened.

Much of it she didn't understand, the world outside the
Heartspace of the caravans was strange and unknown to her

but a determination, an emotion she had not felt since she'd abandoned the task of attempting to win praise from her grandmother's lips, filled her spirit.

I won't forget you or what you've done for me, she said silently to the ghost of Starmaster Vendran, her hand tightening around the cora'stone. *I promise on my mother's memory, and the memory of Nemisdrillion. I will learn; I will do all that I can.*

Taking a breath, Iana held close the fire that had stirred within her heart and hurried after Arais to a future she had never imagined.

FROM THE AUTHOR

Dear reader,

I truly hope you enjoyed *Starbinder*. It's my absolute pleasure to have been able to offer you this novella and give you a glimpse into *The Eye of Eternity* universe.

This novella is set some five hundred years after the Sundering and approximately two thousand years before the events in *The Blood of the Spear*, Book One in *The Eye of Eternity* series proper. In *The Blood of the Spear* we begin to see the future Vendran hinted at, and we do meet Iana again. (Yes, she is still alive in two thousand years' time; the eagle eyed amongst you might have noticed something in the text that speaks to a Shaluay's longevity).

Kaiel Toranth is overflowing with regret. Absent during his mother's final days he is determined to pass the Trials and join the elite Daemon Hunters, hoping to build a safer future for himself and his brother, Darien.

But Athmay still bears the scars of the War of the Summoners, and when an unexpected battle with a daemon reveals Kaiel and Darien's connection to a forbidden Summoner bloodline, they find themselves on the run from friends and foe alike, for at the end of the war, Seers foretold that the Summoners and the daemon hordes would return. And that an Empyros – the most powerful of all Summoners – would be born. If prophecy holds true, then the brothers may hold the fate of the world in their hands...

If you like flawed heroes, edge-of-your-seat action, and intricate world-building, then chances are you'll love the character-driven epic fantasy that is *The Blood of the Spear*.

To those of you who are planning to join the adventure, you have my deepest thanks. I hope that Athmay is a world you can become lost in and return to in the future. And for those of you have already followed Kaiel, Darien, and friends on the first part of their journey, much more is to come.

Yours truly,
Mark.

ABOUT THE AUTHOR

Mark Timmony was born in Sydney and grew up on the Northern Beaches. He's wanted to write for as long as he can remember and has several notebooks filled with illegible scribblings from childhood to prove it. The desire to write led to work as a bookseller and he spent almost a decade working as a genre specialist in Sydney.

You can find him online at https://marktimmony.com/

Lightning Source UK Ltd.
Milton Keynes UK
UKHW011839230822
407666UK00004B/124/J